I0676187

THINGS BELOVED

Two Short Novels

Glenn Morrow

En Route Books and Media, LLC

Saint Louis, MO

⊕ENROUTE
Make the time

En Route Books and Media, LLC

5705 Rhodes Avenue

St. Louis, MO 63109

Contact us at

contact@enroutebooksandmedia.com

Cover Credit: Team Waxwing

Author Photo Credit: Deborah Morrow

Copyright © 2023 by Glenn Morrow

ISBN: 979-8-88870-056-3

Library of Congress Control Number:

2023941167

All rights reserved. Printed in the United States of America. No part of this book may be used or reproduced in any manner whatsoever without written permission except in the case of brief quotations embodied in critical articles or reviews.

Dedication

For my wife Deborah, my best inspiration and
closest reader – Livy, Waxwing, and love of my life.

And for my children and grandchildren,
the moontide that lifts and the wind that directs the
little boat of my imagination.

Disclaimer

This is a work of imaginative fiction. No family members, friends, acquaintances, or public figures appear in these works in any form whatsoever, veiled, fragmented, or otherwise. Any resemblance to any real person, place, or institution is purely coincidental, with one exception. The abstract painting that appears in "The Observatory" is wholly imaginary, but the painter is not. Maxine Yalovitz-Blankenship is a very real artist with works in several galleries, museums, and public installations. Her name is used with her permission and I am honored in this small way to bring her work to your attention.

Acknowledgments

Every writer is myopic. They need the corrective vision of many others to see past their own assumptions and their own ignorance of many things.

I have benefitted from the oversight of fellow writers in Sally Brady's Writers' Group, The Stone House Writers' Workshop, the Willett Free Library Writers' Group, and others. These include: John Altobello, R.C. Binstock, Chris Cassaday, Bob Dutson, Pam Floyd, Alice Holstein, Anna Kovel, James Lansill, Kiki Latimer, Jeffrey Lewis, James Morrow, Kate Risse, and Larry Rothstein.

Sally Brady has nurtured my writing for years and I gratefully acknowledge her influence in every clear sentence.

My brother Chris Todd Morrow gave me the invaluable perspective of the common reader. He and Donald Bennett (of *Courageous* and *Beagle*) also saved me from many nautical disasters. The several errors that have undoubtedly persisted are entirely mine.

Sebastian Mahfood and Kiki Latimer were instrumental in getting this work into print.

Table of Contents

The Observatory

1

For the present, the observatory dome sits atop Astronomy Hill, fourteen miles due east of the campus. I was one of hundreds driven in a college van across the pitch-black desert, dozing our way back to the freshman dorms, heads dizzy with the rings of Saturn. I was one of dozens who returned with sleeping bags for Optical Astronomy 101, taking my shift at the eyepiece while on the far side of the dome half the football team slept. OA-101 was considered a "gut," with the added benefit of freeing up practice time during daylight hours. And I, Josh Redford, was one of six who majored in OA, captivated by the light of distant bodies. When you're a freakishly tall science geek with a serious nocturnal habit, it helps to have friends on the football team.

What brought me back here was an alumni fundraising email, one of hundreds that I hadn't read over the intervening decades. But this one was texted to me by Kirk, so I paid attention. It referred to the "competitive educational environment" and the necessity of "hard choices." Kirk's subject line translated succinctly: "They're selling the dome."

I texted back to Kirk: "Meet me @ dome Sunday night."

"We already plan sat nite. full moon."

"We?" I texted.

"Sat nite," replied Kirk, "get key."

Old Prof. Philbrook's office was eerily empty since his retirement: corkboard and thumbtacks; tattered map of the moon; a table of Cepheid variable stars, those "standard candles" by whose consistent pulsing light we measure vast distances. Time and space. The observatory key was right where I expected – top right-hand drawer.

I drove the desert in the autumn dusk toward that one unlikely hill rising from the flat. Every OA alumn knows the alarm code: 72169. The date Neil Armstrong's boot hit the lunar dust.

I was there before the others, alone in the cold dome, staring at this beautiful ungainly beast of brass and glass in the red safety light. Twenty-five years older and both of us obsolete.

Between the observatory and the photography darkroom, I'd spent a good part of my youth in red-lit darkness. There's a fascination that comes when you realize that taking a photo is just the beginning of seeing. There's always more that develops in the printed image than what was in front of your eyes.

The rest of them should be here soon. Kirk, of course, the only one I had kept in touch with, smarter than you'd expect from a middle linebacker. And the others he mentioned: Howie of the endless puns, Raj whose family pride in an astronomy major was up for endless re-negotiation, and Rita, queen of the spectrograph, who we all were in love with in our secret nocturnal hearts so many years ago. Dreamers all, with the precision that such dreams required.

Soon is a relative term when you're standing in a chilly concrete observatory. I hadn't seen any of my fellow astronomers in decades, scattered without pattern to the four corners of a continent. I considered turning on the bright lights, but decided to keep the red, let our eyes adjust.

Howie was the first to arrive, as predictable as old Neil's 'one small step' with his opening line: "Friends, roaming countrymen, lens me a near." Howie is balding now and wears a bushy flourish under his nose, as if to say 'look down here, not up there.'

We gave each other the Vulcan salute "Live long and prosper." Cheezy as hell, but there's a comfort in old rituals, however debased. Then even Howie fell silent in contemplation of the big brass Zeiss.

But, being Howie, his silence didn't last long. "What are they going to do with it?"

"Nobody seems to know."

"Is that the Nobody who doesn't know, or the Nobody who knows and won't say?"

We let the question hang in the hilltop air, hushed in the ruby lighting that kept the blackness at bay while preserving our night vision.

Raj was next to arrive. "Long life and prosperity." A mechanical genius, Raj's brilliance never quite made its way to the language centers of his brain. Which made him impervious to Howie's puns. Raj would never say that he invented the 3D printer, but the alumni news reported a long string of patents. His company is highly respected in Maker Hacka-thons, in Big Med labs printing artificial heart valves, and in secret basements where deposition jets print undetectable plastic guns to put holes in those hearts.

Though Raj could never acknowledge it, all technology, even his, is double-edged.

"Well," said Raj, "being here, should we not have a look see?"

We were trespassing, of course. Everything we were doing could and probably would be held against us in a court of law. But the night has its own rules. I hit the button to open the dome.

"Wait just a darn New York minute" came a booming voice, ricocheting around the lively acoustics of the dome. Kirk. "Opening the kimono is my job."

"Can we can the kimono thing once and for all?" said Rita, "Honestly. If these walls could speak, the amount of sexual innuendo in this observatory..."

"We met at the airport," explained Kirk, "shared a rental car."

"Oh, that Hertz." Howie, of course.

"Can we perhaps get some rotation here?" said Raj.

"Coming right up."

The night sky swiveled until we slotted on the moon, pale as a wine cracker over the Sonoran.

"It's beautiful."

"Mr. DeMille, I'm ready for my close-up," quoted Howie.

"Ladies first," said Kirk.

Rita gave him the "whatever" shrug and climbed into the bucket. Using the two hand controls she pivoted with the telescope until it aligned with the slotted moon, the long brass tube like a path of reflected light on night water. Rita pushed back her ebony curls and put her eye to the lens, making minute adjustments with old muscle memory, soaking in moonlight.

Each of us took a turn at the dioptric, gazing at our companion satellite which keeps half of herself forever hidden from our view. We spoke in whispers. We fell into the old Latin, calling out the *Mons* and *Mare*, no "Sea of Tranquility" for us. We could have gone all night.

Suddenly a sound like a gunshot ricocheted around the dome.

"I brought champagne," said Kirk.

"Surely you know the moisture rules in proximity to the lenses." Raj, naturally.

"I thought tonight we could be a little flexible." Kirk poured out five plastic glasses and made a toast to our telescope. "To old Wilkins."

"A refractor to remember!"

We sipped champagne, cold and sparkling as the night sky.

"Do we know what the plans are for her?" said Rita, pointing at the telescope. A long silence.

Kirk explained. "There's a wealthy Angelino who wants a second home on a hilltop with a view."

"This hilltop already has a heavenly view," said Howie, gesturing at the stars.

"I think they view this dome as a problem."

"They cannot do this thing," said Raj.

"They can and will," I said, "Unless someone else can come up with as much money as the college will get for the site." I cast a long apprising look around the room at a successful entrepreneur and a former professional football player. Howie pulled out his wallet and started counting single dollar bills.

"We're a day late and a dollar short," said Kirk. "The college has already accepted an offer. If we had legal status, we could tie it up in the courts. But we're just alumni."

"Alumna!"

"We wouldn't win, but we could hire some lawyers. But the college isn't selling Astronomy Hill because they got tired of the commute. They're selling it because they're in serious financial trouble, like a whole lot of other small private colleges. They regard this sell-off as a lifeline."

Each of us fingered our empty plastic flute.

"But surely someone wants this telescope," said Rita.

"People. Wake up and smell the frozen methane," said Howie. "Ground-based optical astronomy is dead. Finished. Even in Finnish they say it's finished. Nobody wants a second-hand refractor. Unless your name is Hubble or James Webb, you've got no business looking at the stars anymore. There's nothing left to see. This place had its day. But nowadays this telescope is just an optical aberration."

"Aberration?" said Raj, "this is obscure."

"But the Wilkins telescope?" said Rita.

"Bulldozed with the rest of this rubble."

"They cannot do this thing," said Raj. He crossed his arms. Despite the dim red light, I could see a tear.

An observatory isn't just a telescope in a dome. It's one big, interconnected machine, one that brings close an image and splits it off to many destinations, not just to the eye, but to a bestiary of devices that see better than we do. The human eye is pretty limited, actually, and has an annoying tendency to see things that aren't there, like canals on Mars.

The last holdout of 19th century science, optical astronomy could measure and categorize and compare, but we were powerless to run experiments on the universe. "Cause it's the only universe we've got", as Howie put it. We learned our constellations and learned to distrust the seductions of their seemingly adjacent clusters of stars. Professor Philbrook drummed it into our brains that the cosmos isn't the way it happens to look from here: apparent isn't real.

By our second semester, we barely looked at the stars. We compared spectrums for elements and archives of photos for discrepancies. But still the Observatory was there, and we travelled here like pilgrims to a shrine to confirm that behind all the data there was something real and eternal, something out there.

"I am married now. I have a son," said Raj, "I want him to be able to come here. He needs to see the stars."

"I bought the twins a telescope for their 10th birthday," said Rita. "Backyard astronomy. It gathers dust, not starlight. The night sky asks more patience of us than anyone has these days."

"That is precisely why this place is needed," I said. "Howie is right, the scientific world doesn't need this old telescope. But we do. This place gives occasion to patience."

"Apparently patience is an elective that the college has opted to drop from the syllabus," said Howie.

"The college is in trouble. We all know that. Increased costs, diminishing pool of applicants. Astronomy never was a big draw."

"The football team liked it a lot. Most of us."

"What I'm saying is you can't blame the college."

"You most certainly can," said Rita. "There's a whole galaxy of colleges out there. Precious few have an observatory. Half of the handful that do are squinting through light pollution and road vibration that didn't exist when they were built. This place is a gem. The college just didn't market what they have."

"A crown without a jewel is just a hat," quipped Howie.

"Had. What they marketed is a hilltop level building site with road access and electricity," I said. "In realtors' terms what we have here is a tear-down."

"Like the paper towel dispensers say 'Pull down. Tear up'," Howie, of course. "The college thinks it's disposable, and they've washed their hands of it."

It was cold inside the dome, colder than I remembered. Maybe we just have older bones and the chill gets in more.

"I don't have any kids to send here," said Kirk. "I had a wife who loved the glamor of the League, my name on the backs of the fans. She didn't understand the repetitions, the meditation on doing the same thing over and over and over until your body changes to become that thing. It was this place, more than the field or the gym, that taught me that time moves at its own pace. To be patient with it."

I thought about my own journey. I was a photographer when photography meant something. The darkroom skills I learned from OA came in handy, while there were still darkrooms. When it all went digital, I found a new niche, pixel scanning all those suddenly obsolete silver halide images and then click by click retouching them – initially just filling in scratches and taking out the red eye, then gradually making them realer than real. Enhancing became a full-time job. People wouldn't believe how many of the photos they see every day have been "touched" – just about everyone and everything looks just a little better than it really is. When there's no negative, the changed image just gets copied over the original.

My name is written into the contracts of certain models because I know what they consider imperfections and what is required. Skin smoothing and flyaway hairs, of course, but also removing neck muscles, ear lobes, and that philtrum groove between the nose and the upper lip. I've been completely erasing the collarbones of one famous model for years. Of course, the contracts never say exactly what I'm doing, it's all "image consultation".

"I don't have kids either," I said. "I've mostly dated fashion models – trust me Howie, there's nothing sexy about it – and they're not interested."

Flooding the Plössl eyepiece with light, the Moon was full and round. She can't be improved. She is a non-stop map of imperfections, craters and scars. And she's perfect.

Riding the bucket in moonlight, I snapped a photo of the Mare Serenitatis and heard the camera click. First photo I've taken in months. I wondered if it would be the last image this telescope would ever take, and whether it would ever be developed. If it is, it's evidence that we were here. That and the lost champagne cork.

"What we need is a good lawyer," said Kirk.

"Oxymoron," said Howie.

"A lawyer could buy this observatory time. Bury the bulldozers in legal paper. Purchase enough time for the college to get back on its feet. Delay enough to frustrate the developer into looking for a less complicated building site, a Plan B. Then the college could re-purchase Wilkins."

"That's a lot of ifs," said Rita, "If we had a case. And a really clever lawyer. And a sympathetic judge. And all that time and money. Why is it when people hit forty they suddenly develop faith in lawyers? I think that if we love this place, we should defend it. Not pay someone else to do it."

"Direct action?" said Raj, looking a little stunned by the idea.

"'Occupy Astronomy Hill.' It has a nice ring to it," said Howie.

"And utterly impractical. What are we going to do? Chain ourselves to the telescope?" I asked rhetorically. "We're not student radicals anymore. Tell the truth, I don't think any of us ever were. We're responsible adults with lives, and families, and jobs to go back to."

"Direct-ish then. What kind of buildings can't be torn down?"

"Historic sites."

"Kirk Stolkolski slept here!"

"Not historic enough, I'm afraid. If only someone had made a really important discovery here, like Clyde Tombaugh finding Pluto."

"Or NASA finding Houston."

"Pluto isn't even a planet anymore." We wrangled back and forth about Pluto's demotion. Howie lining up with Kirk for the traditionalist argument. Raj and Rita taking the side of the International

Astronomical Union that size does indeed matter. I satisfied nobody by arguing that the whole enshrining of planets over-simplified a solar system full of irregular objects. It felt like old times.

"Endangered species," said Raj.

"Don't be ridiculous. Pluto is not endangered."

"No. I meant here. This hilltop they cannot bulldoze. Not if it is a nature preserve."

"A lizard sanctuary?" said Howie, "I don't think so. Has anyone ever noticed any rare or threatened creatures up here? Astronomy students excepted."

"We mostly came up here at night. But this is a good line of thought," said Kirk. "Anything else?"

"Tribal lands? A traditional sacred site?"

"Even if it was, which it isn't, that almost never works."

"Archeological site?"

"Only after it's a ruin."

"Hazardous waste site? These pivot bearings are floating on a pool of vibration-dampening mercury."

"Yeah, but it's well contained. That just means they're going to have to rip it apart *carefully*. That's the only way to get those ruby slippers."

Howie looked over at Raj, who obviously didn't get the reference. That's more than half of why Howie does it. To watch Raj miss the bus.

"I've got one more," I said. "Active crime scene. They can't demolish an active crime scene."

"The only crime here is the one that some real estate developer is about to commit," said Kirk.

"Unless, of course, we can kill him first. Professor Philbrook in the Observatory with the Wrench," added Howie, not particularly helpfully.

"This isn't a game of Clue," said Rita, "and we're not even board game detectives. We're just a bunch of people who spent a few semesters many years ago doing the most passive thing we could imagine, looking through a portal to heaven. Watching things happen that we had no ability to change. Aren't we doing the same thing now? The only difference is that now we're middle-aged and our portal is nostalgia. If the worth of this telescope is what it was in some hazy past, then I agree with Howie – let it go."

Raj raised a finger, which has always been his way to signal objection.

It was in that moment that I really saw Rita. Not as beautiful, in some late-night only-girl-in-the-room way. Not because she was also really smart, as if smart were the other piece of the puzzle. I saw her as honest.

"The only value of this observatory" continued Rita "is what it will be. What it can teach children about themselves. That's what lasts. That's what's worth fighting for."

"Listen," said Kirk. "When I walked inside the dome with that silly bottle of champagne, I saw something, something I didn't want to say to any of you. What I saw was how small Wilkins actually is. I expected to be awed by its majesty. I wasn't.

"The first time you're on a football field in a stadium full of cheering fans, you feel big. Immense. You're a star. Thankfully, that doesn't last. What you come to realize is that it's the field that's immense. There are too many yards. You gain and lose every single one over and over like trench warfare. You're not a hero. You're just an X or an O that goes somewhere out into that immensity. A map of the stars."

"Humility. Patience. A sense of wonder," said Raj. "It doesn't take a big telescope."

For the first time that evening, we were all silent. Five old friends. Scattered by the years. Re-united in that moment.

"I've never had any complaints about the size of my telescope," said Howie. "Speaking of which, I'll be right back. I gotta go uncork a couple glasses of that champagne."

"Pee on the dome, not in the dome," an old astronomy class phrase that sprang from my lips without so much as a conscious thought.

"Guys. Really?" said Rita.

Howie left the Observatory. I imagined him out there in the pristine dark, miles from light pollution, pissing on the ground and gazing up at the Milky Way.

Then Howie was back in the Observatory. He jumped through the door and yanked the handle down behind him.

"There's someone out there."

"What?"

"There's a guy out there. Leaning against the dome."

Kirk blitzed across the Observatory like a line of scrimmage and hit the button to close the dome aperture.

"Subtle," I said in an echoing whisper.

"I'm sure that will convince him that there is nobody here," said Raj.

And then we were talking in whispers not of awe but of secrecy.

"Who was it? Was it the campus cops?"

"I dunno. Don't think so. No uniform, if that's what you're asking."

"Maybe he didn't see us."

"Um. We've got cars in the parking lot."

"Well, maybe he's just some random traveler who saw the dome, decided to take a closer look."

"We're hardly on the way to anywhere."

"We could act like we're supposed to be here. Bring him in, give him a peek through Wilkins."

"That would be a great idea if he's the cops."

And so we debated in stress-hushed voices. Professor Philbrook? Hamlin come to join us after all? Howie only got a glimpse in the moonlight, but neither seemed likely. Finally, Kirk turned to me and said, "Josh, we think that you should go out and talk to him."

"We?"

"Yeah. We all think you're the best choice."

I didn't know whether to feel flattered or scape-goated. But there's no arguing with Kirk. I know, I've tried. He listens patiently, expresses interest in your arguments, then invariably goes ahead with his initial decision. At some point years ago I realized that his hearing you out has nothing to do with being influenced by your opinion; he's evaluating your mental readiness to be put into the game.

I took a deep breath, ducked my head through the doorway, and stepped outside the observatory.

The man was still there, leaning his back against the curvature of the dome. Waiting me out.

"Hi," I said.

"Beautiful night."

"Full moon."

"Oh yeah. You're right. Hadn't noticed." He then lapsed into silence, which allowed me to observe him. Tall, silver-haired, patrician. His dress was oddly nautical. Maybe that works in the penetrating cold-ness of the desert night air.

"What amazes me," he said, "is that this whole structure has no insulation. I've checked. None whatsoever."

"Probably because there's a big slot opening in the roof?"

"Yeah. That makes sense, I guess. But not very useful."

"Except for what it was designed to do."

"By that," he said, "I assume you mean gawking at things that can have no possible effect on our lives. Colossal waste of time and concrete if you ask me."

I hadn't asked him. But I had a pretty good idea of where he was coming from.

"Did you know that an asteroid the size of, say, that Mercedes over there, crashes into the Earth's atmosphere about once a year? And then there's one called Toutatis that looks like a cave man's idea of a bowling pin. It's no Mercedes. It's a couple of miles long, solid rock, and it crosses our orbit every four years. Kept a lot of people awake in 2004."

"Far as I'm concerned," the nautical gentleman replied, "if there's an enormous rock up there with my name on it, I'd prefer not to know."

Hunh. Maybe I didn't know where he was coming from.

"Asteroids. Solar flares. Space junk. Feels to me like some new form of prognostication. Forecasting nothing but bad weather with no umbrellas. You can save me your comets and your moon rocks. I don't see the point."

"Curiosity?"

"Killed the prospects of more otherwise smart men than it ever killed cats. College kids come out here and gawp at the rings of Saturn. Can't imagine a bigger waste of human potential."

"So you'd rather remain in the dark?"

"Actually, it's you folks that are in the dark. Night after night. I mean, you've got to admit it's a little weird, an occupation that can only be pursued in the middle of the night. Waste of a perfectly good night is my opinion. From the cavemen on up, the nighttime was the time for conviviality. Getting together to eat and drink, make music, dance, make love. And then sleep. Only the misfits, the outcasts, the wolf bait went off alone out of the safety of the cave into the darkness. To stare at stuff that could have no possible effect on their lives. Then making up stuff – astrology – to claim that it did."

"We don't believe in astrology."

"I'm sure you don't, professor,"

Professor?

"...but you believe in something just as absurd. That what's happening millions of light years away is somehow important. And you find young impressionable kids who are too dazzled to realize that no matter how 'scientific' it is, it really doesn't matter a damn. And beyond their little circle, people might pretend to care about it. But they won't. Not really."

I leaned back against the dome and thought of all the times I'd mentioned my degree in Optical Astronomy. A real conversation stopper.

"So," I said, "with all of that feasting and lovemaking going on, why are you out here by yourself in the middle of the night in the middle of nowhere leaning against this big badly-insulated concrete dome."

"I have my reasons. Let's say I'm prospecting."

He turned away from me then, apparently feeling that we had nothing further to say. He set his yachtsman's cap, zipped the high collar of his storm jacket tight around his neck. Then he pulled out his cell phone and stared at it incredulously, unable to take in the fact that there is no cell service whatsoever out here. He punched at the little screen a couple of times, then restored it to his pocket.

"You can tell your students that they don't have to hide in there. I'm not the wolf. I don't bite."

Somehow this landlocked mariner had mistaken me for Old Philbrook. "They're not students. At least not anymore."

"Well, I'm sure they're not dancing or lovemaking in there. Your precious obsolete telescope wouldn't take well to any of the normal activities of the night."

"You omitted one. We tell stories."

"Whatever."

So I called the gang out. The first to emerge was Kirk. Never exactly the shy retiring type, he came through the observatory door establishing eye contact, hand extended for the shake. "Kirk Stolkolski."

"Yes," said the mariner in the desert, pretty cool for someone encountering a middle linebacker in the moonlight. "Minnesota Vikings, wasn't it?"

"Baltimore Ravens. Same color jerseys. Purple and white."

Couldn't have been a clearer example of Kirk's late-night complaint about being 'all-pro semi-famous.'

"So," said Kirk, "I didn't catch your name."

"Milken"

"As in The Junk Bond King?"

"My father."

"Didn't he..."

"Receive a Presidential Pardon? Yes."

I suspect the only thing that could have broken Kirk's prolonged handshake was what happened next. Rita emerged from the observatory and exclaimed "Geoffrey?"

Howie was right behind her, but light years behind the situation. "You know this guy?"

Neither dignified his unnecessary question with an unnecessary answer.

"We met," said Rita, "at Peggy Noon's. 'Good Works and Good Work.'"

"Always hated that slogan."

"They were selling a Blankenship."

"THE."

"OK, *The* Blankenship. It made the hairs on the back of my neck prickle," said Rita. "I wanted it because, well, I wanted it. And it was my birthday." Rita noticed our blank expressions. "An abstract painting by Maxine Yalovitz-Blankenship."

Rita searched each of our faces for a glint of recognition. We were glintless. She attempted to explain: "It's called *Georgia Moon*. There's a moon, sort of. It's misty, a memory. And there are these small bright shapes floating in the picture plane. At first glance the canvas is flat. Then the colors start to push and pull each other. These spots of color catch and redirect your gaze. The visual path accelerates. It opens up an enormous depth and your eye falls in. The zero-point perspective somehow twists as it recedes. You're going somewhere in there that's both deeply comforting and very far away. Like I said, horripilation." The expressions around me in the moonlight didn't appear any less blank.

"It's an appreciable non-fungible investment vehicle," said Geoffrey. "But the birthday thing was important. So, here's the deal."

"We both wanted it. But it was my birthday."

"Her husband Chet joined us during negotiations and said 'Happy Birthday' with a big grin. He went pale when he saw the price tag. That made it obvious they couldn't afford it. So, I proposed a joint conservatorship. Chet didn't have much choice but to sign the check."

"What Geoffrey means is we both bought it," said Rita. "Total strangers. We went halfsies. I got to take it home and hang it on my living room wall; he got all the paperwork – the authentication, the provenance…"

"I retained titular ownership of record."

"See, my husband Chet is big on birthdays. I mean Big. On his birthday he gets what he never had as a child…"

"Rosebud."

"That's not fair. But he does get a piñata, a magician, balloons and hats, cake and ice cream," said Rita. "The twins have made it easier. They, of course, love it, and aren't quite old enough to realize that most adults don't have a petting zoo for their 47th birthday.

"And on my birthday, Chet gives me whatever I want. Well, in this case, half of what I wanted. Half a

Blankenship is still plenty expensive, but for Chet every birthday is special, and this was a big round one."

"The one thing I appreciate about art is that it appreciates" Milken interrupted. "People value most what they fear they are about to lose – like an artwork in an auction. Human nature. So they bid the price up. Once they've got it home the luster fades. They redecorate. It doesn't match the couch. Eventually they want to sell."

Rita gestured a protest at this. It was clear that his idea of art and hers were worlds apart. Milken ignored her and went on.

"The transaction had some involvements. The way Chet and I wrote it, when the Blankenship is sold, they get their half of the money back, I get my half – and all the appreciated profits. Cheaper than a vault."

"So," Kirk mused, "in this kind of art deal, one of you has possession but the other has a huge on-field advantage. Interested to see how it plays out."

At this point Raj came through the Neil Armstrong doorway. "Someone left the spectrograph running, doing a multi-factorial analysis of the inside of the dome… Hello?"

"This is Geoffrey," said Rita. "He owns the Observatory."

"And you are Raj Chatterjee, CEO of Accretion Systems," said Milken extending a handshake. "Very pleased to meet you."

"Wait a minute," I said. "You obviously know Rita, you recognized Kirk, and apparently you know who Raj is too?"

"I do my homework. Sorry about the team, Kirk. Baltimore Ravens."

We were all quiet then, bathed in the cold bleach white of that full moon's light. I can't speak for Howie, but I think that all of us realized the same thing at the same time. This was not some random real estate transaction, some hilltop-house-in-the-desert dream. Milken knew that Rita had been an astronomy student here.

Rita could have that effect on men. My first thought was to envision Milken girdling the observatory with a birthday ribbon and presenting Rita with it. But that mental image was mercifully fleeting. It might have been something I would do, but I just couldn't conjure Milken having the slightest bit of hopeless romance in him. His only interests seemed to be financial, and he'd set those sights on Raj.

I have to say that my second reaction wasn't very useful either. I was disappointed. And a little annoyed. I wasn't important enough for Milken to factor into whatever he had up his sleeve. "*Professor*"?! I'm pretty well known in my field. A little Google search would have turned up something worth reading, had he really done his homework.

For his part, Howie turned to Milken and gave him the Vulcan salute "Live Long and Prosper." Good old Howie.

Milken kept his gaze fixed on Raj in the moonlight, ignoring the rest of us.

Kirk's optical astronomy was always more dogged than inspired. But from the first he was a natural leader. And he took the lead once again.

"You don't want Astronomy Hill as a construction site."

Milken replied, "No one in their right mind would want to spend a minute they didn't have to staring at the supposed 'view' of this godforsaken desert. With no cell service."

"Right. You want Wilkins – that's what we call the telescope."

"Actually, he kind of hates Astronomy," I volunteered, in case anyone had missed that point.

Raj raised that finger. Kirk ignored him and continued.

"OK, so you don't want a telescope. And you don't want a hilltop in the desert. So what do you want?"

Milken smiled as if to say 'I'm finally talking to an adult.' "It's not what I want, it's what I need."

Kirk had the smarts to wait him out. Milken checked his cell phone, though everyone knew this was just theater.

"No one" he continued "wakes up on their birthday and says, 'What I really, *really* want is a Tax Deduction'." Milken smirked. "Nobody *wants* a tax deduction, but anyone who isn't a complete sucker *needs* one."

"And buying an obsolete telescope…"

Raj with that finger again.

"…off of a struggling non-profit somehow gives you a tax deduction?"

"I guess I'm a pretty bad accountant."

"No, Mr. Milken, I'm confident that you're a pretty good accountant." Kirk never lacked for confidence. "You still haven't told us what you want."

"What I want is to get your attention. You too, Joshua James Redford" Milken gestured at me with his useless cell, "class of '96, currently principal of Enhanced Photo Images, Westport. And I see I've gotten what I want."

"Geoffrey, if this is about forcing me to sell the painting," said Rita, "I don't get it. You must have paid many times what the Blankenship could possibly be worth for this observatory."

"It's not about the painting. Not exactly," said Milken. "The painting is what we'll call a Proof of Concept. There's a gold rush going on nowadays in art. Investing in art. Some of the ugliest damned art you've ever seen. It doesn't matter, no one is actually going to look at it. It's kept in bank vaults. But investors want it because it's non-fungible. You can't interchange one painting for another because each one is unique. At least in theory.

"Of course artists, being artists, have been playing games with fungibility since forever. Any idea how many originals of Rodin's *The Thinker* there are? At least 28. Nobody is quite sure. He made quite a few of them after he was dead.

"Rita, if it were about the painting, I could hire an art student to paint a copy of it. Art students work cheap. Then if I put it on the market as a reproduction or a copy, *no problemo*. But if I claim it's the original when I sell it, then I've crossed the line into fungibility, and they call the cops on me. They get a bunch of 'Art Experts'," Milken smirked, "and they expose the fraud."

"If you're looking for art experts," said Howie, "you're barking up the wrong tree." Raj gave a blank look. Howie continued. "That dog won't hunt. We're just a bunch of astronomers baying at this big full moon."

Milken kept his back to the moon, which was, indeed, in perigee. "Yet none of you actually became astronomers. You all wised up. I find that reassuring."

"It's a pretty useless degree," admitted Howie.

I thought Milken would take a victory lap with that admission, but, surprisingly, he didn't.

"You did learn one useful skill freezing your butts out here in this dome in the desert. You learned to look at things really, really closely."

"We learned how to look at asteroids, not art," I pointed out, in case Milken had missed the point.

"You used something I believe is called a 'blink comparator'," said Milken.

"Yes," said Raj, "You put two star maps in this device and blink rather quickly from one to the other. The human eye detects very very small differences. It is remarkable."

"And completely exhausting," added Rita.

"And that brings me back to the painting," said Milken. "What if you put the Blankenship on one side of the blink comparator and a really good copy of it on the other side. And then you played Where's Waldo. How long would it take you to notice the differences?"

"Probably a couple of minutes," said Kirk.

"Good eyes, Kirk." I said, "Hard to know. Maybe an hour?"

"What about never," said Milken.

"Never is never easy," Howie replied. "I'd say that art student just earned himself a great big pallet of green."

"But this is not a possible thing," said Raj. "When you make a copy of anything there is loss of information. Introduction of noise. The two cannot be the same."

"You're right. No art forger could make them exactly the same," said Milken. "For one thing, an original painter works fast and a copyist works very very slowly. And their attention is on different things. Eventually it shows. So let's get rid of the art forger."

Raj raised a finger. "Except. The two could be" said Raj "the same. Digital reproduction. No loss of data."

"Exactly," said Milken. "All I need, Josh, is a digital photography specialist. And, Raj, an expert in 3D printing. Make me my own perfect copy of the Blankenship. I'll give it to myself for my birthday. And I'll give you back your precious telescope."

"Back?" said Rita.

"A big donation to your alma mater. And a nice tax deduction for me. Hell, maybe they'll even put my name on it."

Raj raised his finger of objection. I don't think anyone paid attention but me.

We all looked to Kirk's big round impact-scarred face, our natural leader. He was running the play in his head. "What you're asking us to do is not, legally speaking, illegal?"

"I do not even believe it is technically possible," said Raj.

"Hey" said Milken "You're the technical geniuses. I'm just a money guy. Work it out. Rita has the first painting. She knows where to find me."

"First?" I said.

"Proof of concept."

We watched Milken's red tail lights descend Astronomy Hill. Then we all went back to the dome, punching in with Neil Armstrong's immortal date. We who could endlessly debate Pluto's place in the solar system were unable to start a conversation about a decision that would affect all our lives. We stared at the floor in the dim red light.

"Howie," said Kirk, first to break the silence. "You just found a new hobby. Art supplies. Figure out what Blankenship used. Get the same stuff."

And that's how it was decided.

The moon shone down, but nobody made a move to open the observatory's aperture. Nobody felt much like looking at stars.

2

As Rita told it, Chet didn't say a word about the abstract art suddenly absent from their wall. She told him it was going to my studio because Milken wanted a photograph of it. Her husband had always felt bad because he could only afford half of the painting. And now Rita could only give him half of the truth.

The news from the college Development Office turned increasingly rosy. A hedge fund alumnus who had shown no previous signs of nostalgia made a surprising donation to the general coffers. A loan that was falling due like a cartoon anvil was inexplicably rescheduled. We'd heard nothing from Milken. But to us, at least, it looked like he was pulling strings to keep us motivated.

Howie couldn't paint worth a damn, but he got really good at asking questions about tubes of paint. And by play-acting an artist in need of supplies to tattooed and pierced shop clerks he discovered something surprising. The deep conservatism of art making. Artists – though rebellious in every other way – absolutely *hate* anyone changing their favorite art supplies. So the exact same canvas, gesso, and pigments Blankenship used were still waiting patiently there on the store shelves.

For her part, Rita reverse-engineered the paint, using the office spectrograph to identify in the blended pigments the pure hues Blankenship squeezed from the tubes. And Howie did what Kirk told him to do. He bought lots of paint. But no brushes. Art students working cash registers have surely seen odder things.

I took hundreds of digital photos with carefully calibrated light and precisely recorded angles. When you take a picture of anything you're photographing two things: the object and the light reflecting off the object. Every image of the moon is just a picture of moonshine. That's unavoidable, no matter how subtle the lighting. Unless you take two digital photos with opposite reflective angles and then photoshop out the light. Do that hundreds of times and you end up with an image of the paint itself – how the Blankenship looks in perfect darkness – an impossible photograph. It felt like being back in college again, pulling all-nighters, feeling the floating pieces of something big slowly shifting into place.

Raj was the true hero. He failed and failed and failed again with undiminished optimism. Howie was replicating what had been done. I was doing what I do, enhancing away reality. But Raj, laying down layer upon layer of paint with his 3D printers, was doing something that had never been done before.

I don't think Raj and Kirk had ever been more than acquaintances waiting their turns at the telescope. But in failure and repetition they became brothers. Kirk would listen to Raj go on for hours about matters far, far beyond any of our technical comprehension. Raj would talk and Kirk would listen until Raj knew what he needed to know. Then Kirk would put him back in the game.

And then it was done. The calendar said it was spring, but the cold weather held on like an unresolvable argument. The large thin crate from Accretion Systems had arrived at my studio in Westport. I hesitated to open it until just before the others were due to gather. Sitting by myself for hours with a blatantly obvious failure would have been too painful. I busied myself by nailing two hangers to the wall and trying to decide whether the real Blankenship should go on the left one or the right one.

Finally, ten minutes shy of the time we had chosen to come together, I took the innermost covering off the faux Blankenship and quickly hung it next to the real one. I breathed a sigh of relief. My initial impression was that they were at least twins. I resisted the temptation to examine more closely. This was the first real test. Could our creation fool us, its creators? I took my place in the outer office so I could bring my fellow Optical Astronomers in one by one.

Howie was the first to arrive. He held up his hand in the spread-fingered Vulcan salute. His weeks in the depths of art supplies had supplied him with an even more flamboyant moustache.

"I thought you'd go for the Salvador Dali look," I said.

"Been done. I was thinking more Tycho Brahe," he said fingering his luxuriant upper lip. "So. Where are they?"

"In here. Vote for the real one and keep your vote secret from the others."

"Jeez," said Howie. "I thought the new paint would be brighter. But the colors… Josh, this is a miracle. I can't tell them apart." He stared at the two paintings for a good twenty minutes, shifting from one leg to the other, looking for something he couldn't find. Finally, Howie shrugged then smiled conspiratorially like he had cracked the code. And picked the wrong one.

Kirk and Raj arrived together. I took their coats, then one by one ushered them into the inner room.

Since I alone knew which was which, I stayed in the background, trying not to influence my friends.

Kirk started at the top left corner and systematically compared the two paintings as a collection of parts, his head bobbing back and forth. He picked the real Blankenship but told me it was a coin flip.

Kirk thumped Raj on the back as they passed in the doorway. I hoped that he hadn't tipped off Raj with some gesture or glance. I needn't have worried. Raj was determined to find the limits of his technology. He moved lights around. He looked at the paintings edge on. He focused on one suspect spot as if it were a black hole whose gravity he was unable to escape. I eventually had to force him to make a choice. He chose the fake.

"Judging by our expressions, we're all pretty clueless about which is hanging on which *clou*," said Howie. "I don't even think it's about real and fake anymore."

"Elaborate, please," said Raj.

"You see two stars out there, and they're absolutely identical. Like no two stars are ever identical," said Howie. "Know what you got? 'Twinkle twinkle / gravity lensed / How I wonder / what you bend?'"

"I think the way it goes is not that," said Raj.

"So you gotta ask yourself which one is the real star. Wrong question, Raj, because your best answer is: 'both.' Or maybe 'neither.' What you're seeing is the light from one star split into two images by that big ol' gravitational lens. Neither one is more real than the other."

"Are you saying that neither one of these is the real Blankenship anymore?" said Kirk.

"I think *you're* saying that. I'm just killing time waiting for Lovely Rita spectrometer maid."

Time passed, and Rita didn't show. I became more and more aware that she hadn't phoned or texted. Rita was the most important vote. Only she had lived with the painting. The painting moved her, it had meaning beyond its pigments and technical specs. For her it contained a sea of emotions within its four canvas corners. Would our deception awaken that in her, or would it be as flat as a wedding photo of strangers?

I began generating more and more complex hypotheses based on nothing, like I was Percival Lowell charting the canal system of Mars. Was what we have done a betrayal? Did making a perfect copy of her painting destroy the original for her? Though we had done nothing illegal, had we, in trying to save the observatory, committed a crime against Rita?

I looked around at my fellow criminals. And we had all grown up. In the light of this pair of paintings we had suddenly become adults in a way that aging and responsibilities had failed to do. We had succeeded, and in the heart of success seen our deeper failing. And then Rita arrived.

"Sorry we're late," she said.

We. She stepped into the outer office with no hint of a shadow, as sunny as if this was her birthday and she was getting not half a painting, but a whole one.

Milken would get his copy and she would take her Blankenship home for good. The street door closed and then opened again. Her husband Chet joined the Optical Astronomy class of '96.

"He's lived with the Blankenship as long as I have. I couldn't not tell him," said Rita. "Besides, we might need a tie-breaking vote."

Rita and Chet went in together and closed the door behind them. They were in there a long time. Raj hovered nervously. The reproduction was his creation, we were mere fallible assistants. The thing that we had always admired about Raj was the same thing that drove us crazy: he is a perfectionist. Good isn't good. Good is a socially acceptable deception, the B+ given to people who want to move on. For Raj only the perfect was true, and so he had willed into being a perfect replica. But in its making there was never an intent to deceive. "Why did I not put in a clue?" he said rhetorically. None of us had an answer.

Rita and Chet came out with their arms around each other, holding each other up. The sunshine was gone. Howie wanted to tally their votes but hesitated when he saw their tears.

"Imagine," said Chet, "you went into your only child's bedroom and there were two of them sleeping there, identical, side by side. Your perfect daughter and a perfect stranger. And you unable to tell them apart. You told one of these children a bedtime story and kissed her goodnight. But now you realize that you'll never know which one. Everything that your love has memorized in her is now doubled in her twin." Chet glanced at Rita for a confirming nod, then went on. "You have always wanted another child. But not the same child. And yet there they are, sleeping so peacefully. And you are terrified to wake them up."

"Because you know in that instant that you have lost both of them," said Rita. "Milken lied to us. He never wanted an undetectable forgery of our painting."

Since that was exactly what we'd spent the last four months doing, we all felt blindsided. And looked it. Raj was the first to regain the power of speech.

"This is not a thing I understand."

Rita stepped out of the protective circle of her husband's arm. She moved into the midst of her friends who had done so much on her behalf so that she could have her painting home again. And all of us could have the observatory. Cake and eat it too. She took a deep breath. Apparently, this wasn't going to be easy.

"Geoffrey Milken's whole existence is measuring risk and gain. There is simply no way that he would risk dealing in art fraud. Not for the few thousands he could get for selling a bogus Blankenship." Anticipating our objections, Rita went on. "Yes, he has the documentation. And no, there would be no reason for anyone to suspect forgery, unless one of us gave the game away. And yes, the replica is even more perfect than we could have imagined.

"The thing is, for Geoffrey to make any real money he would have to do this again and again. And sooner or later he would get caught. Even if the forgeries were perfect. Too many people involved. He knows this. He's always known this."

"But he called this 'proof of concept'," I said.

"Yep," sighed Rita. "We just didn't know which concept."

Kirk weighed in, "So he put us through all this for nothing? Just jerking us around because he had some leverage and liked the feel of doing it?"

"He is truly son of bitch," said Raj, the closest to a swear I'd ever heard from him.

"What about the observatory?" Howie chimed in, his moustache quivering like the shaky handlebars of a two-wheeler ridden for the first time. "Was he lying to us about that too?"

"I don't think so," said Rita. "He wants the painting all right. And he's sincere about trading the observatory for it."

"If he wants the paint-by-numbers hobby kit, we give it to him. What do we care what he does with it?"

"Because we should care," said Chet.

"It doesn't matter whether we give him the original or the copy," said Rita. "Not that anyone but Josh here actually knows which is which. Either painting is worthless to Milken. I should have understood this from the beginning." She was starting to choke up again. "He needs to have both of them."

I felt sorry for Rita, I truly did. Milken had always held legal ownership of the Blankenship, and now he was going to exercise it. She was going to lose her painting. I'd spent enough time with it that I felt I was losing something I too had come to love. But we had to keep our eye on the ball. A painting or two paintings for the observatory? If this was ransom, it was worth it.

"Still there is a thing I do not understand," Raj with his usual prologue. "Mr. Milken cannot sell both paintings. To do so would be the clearest proof of forgery."

"God, you're a bunch of science geeks," an exasperated Rita. "It's not about the thing. Here's what it is: Geoffrey Milken wants both paintings as a proof of concept. The Concept is that no work of contemporary art can be considered unique. Investors, auction houses and galleries stake millions on the fact that an artwork in their possession is one-of-a-kind. That's what makes it valuable. Believe me, it's not because the art speaks to them. Being able to show the right people that he can order up an absolutely indistinguishable copy of any random painting undermines their whole system of art investments. It's dynamite that certain players would be willing to pay Milken almost any amount to keep unlit."

"He's playing with a multi-billion-dollar industry," said Chet.

"Boom," said Rita.

Everyone was silent, as we gathered in front of the two Blankenships. Finally, Raj spoke up. "Then it is fair to assume that we are successful? The two paintings cannot be distinguished?"

It all seemed moot to me, but Raj needed to go through it. I said, "Rita. Chet. Point to the original Blankenship." Their hands wavered back and forth like compass needles, each looking at the other as much as at the artworks. They each pointed. I tallied the final vote.

"Based on your votes," I announced, "the copy we made is slightly more real than the real painting."

"So," said Kirk, "what do we tell Milken?"

Howie raised his hand like we were back in the classroom looking at slides of Main Sequence stars. "That we fucked up? That a child of ten could tell the real from the fake?"

"Even though Milken won't be able to?"

"He's not ten years old."

"And then what?" said Kirk, "He'll give us an 'A' for effort and give the observatory back? Somehow I think that's not going to happen."

"I'm sorry Rita," I said, "When we started this, I thought we were making a forgery so you wouldn't have to own half a painting. But now I see we have to give him both. But you already know that. He'll use your beloved Blankenship to blackmail the art investment industrial complex and get even more obscenely rich in the process. Then maybe he'll give the observatory back."

"Don't we have some responsibility," said Howie "I mean, like to the artists?"

"It's not like the art market hasn't been blown up before," said Kirk. "Someone seems to be doing it continually, usually to prove that moneyed people and institutions are philistines that wouldn't recognize real art if it bit them on the butt. Having hobnobbed with team owners, I can't get too worked up about looking out for the interests of the very wealthy. When our college was teetering on the brink, I didn't see any of them step in with a big donation." Kirk cut a glance at Raj, the only truly rich person in the room.

"Just Milken," said Raj. "He bought property he did not want. Before we even knew it was for sale. And it saved the college. Maybe his was the solitary offer they received."

"What he bought was us," said Rita. "We just didn't know it at the time."

Just then my phone vibrated and a name appeared on the screen: Geoffrey Milken. I picked up the call. He fired off a series of questions about the forgery and the forgers which I tried to answer truthfully. Howie tapped his fingertips against his receding hairline ever more emphatically, silently exhorting me to think. But all the thinking was done. Milken already knew before he picked up his phone that we had what he wanted.

"Three to two? Josh, you set it up, so you couldn't vote. Who was the fifth vote?" said the tinny little voice in the handset, "The birthday boy? Oh, that's perfect. I'll be there Tuesday. By 9:00. No hints. Mine is the only vote that counts." Click.

I laid the phone face down on the table. Howie raised his hand in the Vulcan salute but didn't say the words. Then he shrugged into his bomber jacket and left. The rest of us backed out of the display room to leave Rita and Chet alone with the Blankenships. I looked to Kirk. He threw up his hands. Game over.

Then Raj said, "This is most distressing." He pulled his elegant topcoat from the coat closet.

"Before you go, Kirk, could you provide assistance at the Observatory? There is something rather heavy I need to move."

Kirk rolled his eyes at me. All-pro semi-famous. And Raj sees him as nothing more than muscle on demand. Kirk, my old friend, gives me a goodbye nod and the two leave together.

Chet and Rita were in the inner room, and I was alone at the receptionist desk idly pushing contact prints around. And thinking. The Observatory? If Raj and Kirk are heading to the Observatory, they've got an insanely long drive ahead of them. No. Raj got here using the Accretion Systems corporate jet. OK, a short flight, then a long drive across the desert. Still. It's a big trip. To move something heavy?

Like filling in the fragmentary bits of a dream when you suddenly awake, I started to piece it together. Raj wasn't waiting for Milken. Never intended to. If Kirk wasn't in on it ten minutes ago, he surely was now. The Observatory. Wilkins. The big Zeiss.

It was Kirk's leadership he needed, not his muscle. Raj had already assembled the muscle. He had already rented the heavy equipment. Grand theft optical.

It made no sense at all, and it made perfect sense. Dismounting the big refractor and carting it away to somewhere safe would be expensive. But revenge is cheap at almost any price. Raj could afford it.

Pretty soon Milken would find out that all he owned was an empty dome. And if he wanted to make any trouble about that, Raj had all the evidence in the world to expose Milken's art world fraud, and the technical stature to convince auction houses and galleries that Milken could buy a zillion 3D printers but could never clone another painting. That would require the genius of Raj, and he was no longer for sale.

"Josh?" A voice from the inner room. Rita. I had almost forgotten about Rita and Chet. "You're the only one who knows."

"Sorry. Knows what?"

"Which is the real one," said Rita. "They're truly identical, so it shouldn't matter. But." She hesitated. "I need to know which one is the one that Maxine Blankenship painted. I need to say goodbye to it."

I pointed to the one on the left. I had figured that people would view them left-to-right and assume real to fake. But my friends were clever enough to know that I would think of that, so they'd read them fake to real. One of the many things that Optical Astronomy had taught us is left and right, up and down, have no objective meaning. It could have been Professor Philbrook's motto: 'apparent isn't real.'

Rita and Chet needed their privacy, so I went back out to the reception desk. I thought about the models I'd dated and wished I could call one up now. Just to have someone to talk to who wouldn't understand what I'm saying. But models are like birds in a flock. Unpredictable and abrupt in their actions, intense and specific in their diet, and truly connected only to each other, their companions in migration. Not much comfort there.

Then the front buzzer rang, and it was Raj again. Had he forgotten something? But Raj doesn't forget things. He's whatever the opposite of absent-minded is. Present-minded? I opened the door and he came in, glancing at every corner of the room. "Is Rita here?"

"You just left ten minutes ago. Of course she's still here. In there with the paintings."

"There is this thing I need to show her."

I held up my hand. If Rita had to sacrifice her artwork for us, the least I could do was to protect her from Raj's barging in with some obsessive minutiae.

"Give her a minute."

"No." said Raj, clearly nervous. "I give her this."

Then Kirk was thumping the door with the corner of something heavy. I let him in.

"Digital reproduction," said Raj. "If you make one, why not make two?"

And when Kirk got done unboxing it, there it was. Another perfect Blankenship.

"I did not know if she would want it," said Raj. "Perhaps I presume?"

"Raj, you sly devil."

But Raj saw nothing sly about it. He explained what seemed to him to be obvious. It's a backup. In case there's a problem with the one we are using. NASA always makes two of everything and only shoots one into orbit. Raj was sending one Blankenship out there and needed something near at hand to compare it to. And Raj being Raj, the backup couldn't be a trial proof. It had to be as painstakingly perfect as the first one.

Now was not the time to hand Rita and Chet a consolation prize. I gave a head gesture to Kirk, calling the play. And, like a good middle linebacker, he got it and hustled the third Blankenship into a side room.

"Perhaps I presume?"

"No, Raj, it's a very thoughtful gift. It's just a little too soon." Kirk rejoined us, pulling the door of the consulting room shut. Raj nodded, though it was clear he had no idea what I meant. Raj saw it with the clarity of an equation: Lose something. Replace it as quickly as possible. Minimize duration of sense of loss.

Kirk gave me the international gesture of 'this-was-not-my-idea.'

Chet and Rita had been in there for a really long time. I both dreaded them coming out into this moment and wanted them to emerge and break the tension. Then I had another thought. And I had to ask.

"Raj?" I said. "Are there more of these?"

He looked a little stunned, like an artist who made a painting of a dollar bill and then was accused of counterfeiting.

"Of course, no. That would be wrong."

"You mean unethical?"

"No," said Raj. "Wrong. Mr. Milken was clear on this. Scarcity equals value."

"Actually," corrected Kirk, "he would say uniqueness equals value."

Behind us a door opened. Chet and Rita had finished their farewells. "Kirk. Raj. I thought you two had already left."

"We came back," said Raj unnecessarily, to which Kirk hastily added "Raj needed to check on a detail."

Rita sighed, clearly eager to get away. "No need, Raj. Your work is perfect, damn it." Chet held her coat and Rita squirmed into it. "We have to get back to the twins." Then they were gone.

"So, Raj?" said Kirk, "we've got some miles ahead of us if we want to get to the observatory before nightfall. Shall we?"

I raised an eyebrow and said the obvious "You know that the observatory is now Milken's property. He wouldn't take kindly to any umm..."

"Until he gets his precious paintings Milken isn't likely to quibble about some nostalgic old guys paying a visit," said Kirk.

"Perhaps a bit more than a visit," said Raj. "It is possible you recall how I was convincing to my parents about a degree in Astronomy?"

I did recall. He persuaded them that Optical Astronomy was the only major that would give him unrestricted access to a mainframe computer. Which was true enough, as far as it went. What he failed to mention was that the computer was an antiquated PDP-11. The same obsolete model of computer that MIT had relegated to running its Tech Model Railroad Club.

"The PDP-11?"

"Yes. And is it possible you took note that the PDP-11 is still in use?"

"If it ain't broke, don't even breathe heavily," I said.

And then Kirk brought me up to date. "So Raj here got the idea that while the observatory is offline, so to speak, this would be a perfect time to do a major upgrade. Not just the computer. Bring all the data analytics hardware into the 21st century."

There are moments in life when you doubt that people you've known for years agree with your definitions of simple English words. Perfect time? Milken had staged a hostile takeover of Astronomy Hill, and he hated even the name of the place. With the flick of a cell phone he could have it razed to rubble, or pulled apart and stripped of its assets, like his father had done with countless corporations.

Kirk was reading my face like a concussed teammate.

"Josh. Milken is going to give it back. He will. He'll donate the observatory to the college. It's the only financially smart thing for him to do. That tax deduction."

None of this made any sense. Raj was going to upgrade the observatory? So Milken would get an even bigger itemized deduction? Kirk moved an upraised finger back and forth in front of my eyes, perhaps wondering if I was seeing double, or maybe just cartoon stars and tweeting birds.

It was clear that Kirk felt he needed to spell it out for me. "Josh. We can't wait until he does. We need to do this now."

I managed to get out the word: "Why?"

"Simple. Naming rights."

"I cannot permit this son of bitch to put *his* name on the observatory," said Raj.

"So we're laying the groundwork for a counter-proposal," Kirk said, stuffing his brawny right arm into the sleeve of his jacket. "Two famous alumni. Sizable donation. Milken won't know" – hooking his left arm into the other sleeve – "what hit him."

And then it was just me. Walking from room to room in my empty studio. I was the last link in the chain of custody. I stood for a long time before the two Blankenships hanging side by side. They were truly identical, as Milken had predicted. The one on the left is the original, the one that Maxine Blankenship actually painted. The one that Rita received for her birthday. I took it down off its hook. I got the other replica which Raj just delivered. I hung it on the empty hook. I took the one real Blankenship to the shipping crate in the consulting room and latched the lid down, plunging it into perfect darkness.

Geoffrey Milken arrived the next day. He slowly removed his yachtsman's foul-weather jacket and held it out at arm's length to me. I took it and hung it in the closet. As I returned, he gave me a long apprising look.

To make conversation I asked, "Did you have any trouble finding the place?"

No response from Milken.

"Cup of coffee?"

Somewhere between a tilt of the head and a squint.

"That would be a 'no'?" So much for easy camaraderie. "OK. The paintings are in here. Would you like to see if you can tell them apart?"

"Nope."

I thought that was the whole point of his visit.

"You wouldn't be showing them to me," said Milken, "if they weren't identical. I want you to tell me which one is the original."

"Before you even look?"

"That's my proposal."

And it all started to unravel for me. I had thought, gallantly, stupidly, that I could somehow save Rita's precious painting and return it to her. But my supposedly noble gesture now threatened the entire project. I imagined in my panic that Milken would instantly detect the cheat. He would turn on his heel and walk away, sticking us with the bill. And the observatory would be irrevocably lost.

I threw open the door to the display room and pointed to the painting on the left.

Milken didn't even look. "Josh. Do you play poker?" I allowed that I did. "Don't." said Milken.

He advanced into the room and started scanning back and forth between the two identical replicas: Raj-1 and Raj-2. I stood behind him. It was like being a spectator at a tennis match. With everything you own riding on the outcome. Why did I even try to outsmart this guy? He's just biding his time, making me sweat before calling foul.

"Man. Gotta say you guys did your homework," said Milken "But you shouldn't try to mess with me. The one on the left? I don't think so."

Milken moved back from his detailed inspection, took a foot-forward stance and leaned back, his hand upraised to hold his chin. Like a man play-acting art appreciation. Finally, he pronounced his verdict.

"The one on the right? Definitely the original."

Epilogue

That summer we were all invited to Chet's birthday party. It was a big outdoor affair in their back yard, complete with a small flock of rockhopper penguins. The rockhoppers wandered amongst the guests, begging for fish from iced metal trays. Besides the small raw fish, the rented penguins came with a saltwater wading pool and a keeper wearing a tuxedo t-shirt for the occasion.

The twins, who were emphatically not identical, had recently turned thirteen and had marked the occasion by mastering the eyeroll response to parental behavior. Penguins in their fenced back yard were a challenge to their newfound skill because they couldn't decide whether it was hopeless or really kinda awesome. They compromised by ironically naming the red-eyed waddling birds after various teachers and classmates. The rockhoppers didn't seem to mind.

The Optical Astronomy class of '96 were all in attendance. Kirk arrived with champagne to celebrate Chet's birthday and the restoration of the observatory. Milken, or rather some Cayman Islands shell corporation, had donated Astronomy Hill back to the college. Raj had cut the ribbon on the renovated dome with its sparkling new observing automation system and new Polish/Indian polysyllabic name above the door. At Rita's suggestion, the school featured the dome on the cover of their new promotional literature with the tagline "A small private college with a universe."

A juggler strolled by, casually tossing a shower pattern of three balls and a bowling pin.

"But how did you know Milken would donate the dome back?" I asked Raj. "Since he truly hated astronomy, he might have demolished it, tax deduction be damned."

"This is an interesting thing. The new tech we installed in the observatory? It wasn't property of Milken. It was donated direct to the college. The very moment he broke anything he would be vandalizing college property," said Raj. "Active crime scene."

Whether Milken himself is hiding from justice in the Cayman Islands or busy blackmailing Sotheby's we have no way of knowing. I was the last to see him. I helped him load the two crated faux Blankenships – Raj-1 and Raj-2 – into his car. As he drove away, I waved goodbye to the red tail lights of his Mercedes, my palm open with the middle fingers spread. Live long and prosper.

It was dusk. The hired juggler in whiteface packed up his duffle bag of Indian clubs and his unicycle. He had given Howie three pale blue rubber balls along with a lesson, and now Howie's vast moustache quivered with concentration as he kept the three orbs floating in space. The wading pool was siphoned, and the penguins collected.

Kirk, ever the middle linebacker, intercepted the balls in midair. He gestured Howie toward the house. From the yard we could see the Blankenship glowing in the living room above the couch. The two of them disappeared into the kitchen and returned with the big birthday cake, ablaze with light. "These are Standard Candles," quipped Howie. Raj smiled, in on the joke at last.

Chet made a wish and blew out the constellation of his years. Apparent isn't real. Rita had a further surprise for us all. She brought out the twin's long-neglected hobbyist telescope and set its tripod in the summer grass. Each of us took our turn, gazing up at the stars.

The Better Boat

Dedication

To the memory of Donald LaPorte,
my father-in-law, whose lifetime love of sailing
served as inspiration.

1

She was singing into the wind. With one hand he held the tiller and felt the water fighting back against the wood. The other was gloved and wrapped with the line, taming a boisterous pocket of wind. Twisting his wrist to feel the spill of air into air. The water hissed, the canvas boomed along as she came about. The sky was a painful blue, the sun dodging in and out of the rigging. He could not imagine anything more perfect than this moment. He was twelve years old.

Two months before, wandering the cove he came across a man kicking a boat. The boat was half-buried in sand well above the tidal mark, the bilge filled with greenish rainwater. Anthony watched the man kick the boat. It was worth watching. After several running slams of his construction boots had no visible effect, the boy asked the man why. "The damn town, that's why." The sweat beaded between the hairs of his prickly crewcut. The man stripped off his sweat-shirt and mopped it around over the top of his head. He gave the wooden sailing dingy another couple of kicks, but his heart wasn't in it. Frustrated, he sat on the gunwale and emptied out his discontents. "The damn harbor division won't let us leave it here, violation of mooring regulations. So my mother told me to deal with it. But the damn coastal conservancy won't let me drive anything over the dune to drag it out. And I can't even burn it, the damn fire department doesn't have a variance for that."

"Couldn't you, you know, sail it?"

"Tell you what. If you've got a dollar, it's yours. Ask your dad if he'll sign for you and I'll put her in your name."

"Her?"

"Boats are girls, didn't anyone tell you that? This one's name is Aurora, whatever the hell that means."

The best way to tell if a boat will float is to sink it. Before taking on the week-long task of digging it out of the dune, Anthony filled the stranded dinghy to the gunwales with water and waited for it to run out. Despite the kicks it had received, the hull held. Aboard Aurora for the first time, he scudded imagined seas as he bailed with a sore arm and a Folgers coffee can, thigh-deep in water, sailing on sand.

"It's a catboat, right?" said his friend Francis. Anthony handed him one of the two shovels he'd borrowed, and they set to work.

"Actually," said Anthony, "she's a sailing dinghy. Aurora can carry three sails: mainsail, jib, and I forget what the other one's called. Not that I've got that kind of money."

"Maybe you can get a sail on sale." Francis' first enthusiasm for shoveling sand was visibly slackening. "Aurora, what kind of stupid-ass name is that? I'd call her something like Black Death, or Vengeance, something with pirates in it."

"Aurora's her name. It came with her."

"So?"

"It's bad luck to change the name of a boat."

"Like this isn't already bad luck? Stuck about a zillion feet above high tide? Anyway, from the way you've been talking about this boat all week, you're just about married to it. Don't girls change their names when they get married?"

"It's like your saint's name. Maybe you picked a dumb one, like the priest talked you into 'Aloysius'. So you're stuck with it. And maybe someday you'll find out something really cool about your saint. It's kind of like your mission."

"It's going to take an intercessory miracle to get this dumb boat into the water. Dogboat."

"Keep shoveling."

What it took was a full moon tide to finally get the sailboat off the sand. That, and heeling her so far over that the sand-clogged centerboard rose to their shovels like buried treasure, the mast pulled down as horizontal as a chinning bar. Anthony and Francis pushed against the hull to ride it on edge over the sand, joined by three other guys from school lured by dubious promises of sailing adventures. Anthony had dazzled them with the magical tale of Aurora, his for just one single dollar. He neglected to tell them that his financial horizon was pretty much a blank beyond that and contained not a glimmer of a sail for the dollar dinghy.

Through more luck than anything they got her moving. Aurora slid awkwardly on her flank, sand-papering away what little paint remained on that side of her hull. She reached the tidepool and, buoyant, wanted to right herself. Francis threw his belly across her mast, riding her to keep her sideways. The rest of them whooped and splashed waist-high, pushing her through the sun-warmed water, giddy with flotation. Then at the high tide mark she struck the wet sand like a wall. Abruptly all forward motion ceased. Anthony tried to rally his sand-caked crew to fetch the shovels, and they responded with an unconcealed lack of enthusiasm. At that moment a wave arrived fresh from Portugal, so much higher than the others, to pluck Aurora effortlessly into the surf. There she rode, majestically, Francis wrapped around the suddenly vertical mast, halfway up, like a doughnut on a stick.

Once you have a boat in the water the next thing you have to figure out is how to tether it to the land. Anthony clambered aboard the Aurora carrying two canoe paddles as she bobbed in circles in the surf. The two boys, soaked and sandy, awkwardly paddled her up the cove, hoping that nobody would notice. Of course, the rest of the crew on the beach drew them to everyone's attention, cat-calling useless advice until they rounded the point.

Beyond the rocky point the waves diminished. A concrete pipe under the shore road poured a steady stream of water into the cove. And that's where they tied up the Aurora. The afternoon sun threw the culvert into shadow. It was time to get home for supper. Anthony hoped that his dollar boat would be where he left it, come morning.

At supper his father called him "Skipper" and his mother worried out loud and at length whether this boat thing was safe. She fretted Anthony into the promise that he would never go out sailing by himself. And then they did the things that adults can do that kids cannot. The next morning his father borrowed a motorboat and towed the Aurora to an actual dock a short bike ride from their house. In the days that followed Aurora was outfitted with a mainsail and a three-quarter jib. And loaded down with life jackets and ironclad rules not to be transgressed.

When your uncle introduces you to your first pool table, you quickly learn that the balls you want to sink never ever line up with the pockets. When you get aboard your first sailboat, you discover that the wind never ever wants to take you where you want to go. It seems determined to turn you sideways and push you away. Then by the purest of luck a ball or a wind arrives at just the right angle, and you feel that anything is possible.

Aurora and Anthony soared together, flying over the water on an outstretched white wing. She spoke to him in the slap of sailcloth, the hiss of the bow. He talked to her in terms of endearment. They were like friends that knew all the same things, best buddies that completed each other's sentences. Francis, his actual best buddy, sat low in the hull in his orange life preserver, looking a little green and mostly keeping out of the way. Then the wind collapsed. Anthony's father came up alongside with the noise and fumes of a borrowed outboard motor and towed Aurora slack-sailed back to the dock.

He had to make a lot of the stuff himself. Anthony's first tiller was a hockey stick handle attached with 6 penny nails. Just nailed it to the rudder post. Experience will teach you. One good following sea and the tiller came off in his hand. Behind the sputtering outboard Aurora wallowed back to the dock, the sea sparkle cackling out his disgrace. So he learned joinery. Tiller and rudder. Wood locked to wood, each bends as the other bends. Being of one substance, as they said at Mass.

And then over dinner Anthony's mother said "Your cousin is coming to the shore for a couple of weeks. To stay with us. Maybe help you with the boat. You know, crew."

It's a treacherous word, "cousin". Especially if you have a lot of them. It doesn't tell you anything that you need to know. All it tells you is that you have to put up with them for as long as they end up staying. I mean, some cousins are great, nothing against them. Cousins that are close to your age. Otherwise, you either get a tag-along or a bored teenager who wishes he wasn't there and fills his time thinking up mean tricks to play on you.

"Sure, Mom." And that's all the illumination Anthony got on the subject.

Since there's no arguing with the duty to entertain cousins, he took it up with Francis. Sometimes he's got good ideas.

"Man, I just hope for your sake that it's not a girl cousin." That horrible thought hadn't even crossed his mind. "Some of your cousins are girls, aren't they?" Anthony started counting on his fingers.

"Yeah, I think so."

"Be just your luck, Anthony. The problem with girl cousins…" They both knew what the problem with girl cousins was. "…well, aside from the fact that they're girl cousins. The other problem is that they can never see how awesome anything *is*. They only care how awesome things *look*."

"Yeah. Where did girls end up with the notion that everything has to look good?"

"I think they teach them that. Probably in CCD," said Francis.

"Hey." Anthony said, "you want to take the Aurora out?"

"You just like me because I weigh more than you do."

He had no idea where Francis was going with that. But OK. "You don't weigh much more than I do."

"Do too. Lots more."

"So?"

"So the next time the wind capsizes you, you want my weight standing on the centerboard to get the wet sails out of the water."

"Yeah? That's part of sailing, Francis."

"But it's the part where I get dunked twice. Once when you screw up and let the boat flip, then when I get you upright I end up butt first in the drink again. And the stupid dogboat sails away from me and I gotta swim for it."

"You're supposed to hang on."

"Right. Let's see you try it."

Anthony and Francis took Aurora out. There were little puffs of wind, and though it didn't actually take them in the direction they wanted to go, it did take them up the cove to where the fancy sailboats waited in the marina for something more than whiffy scraps of air. He let Francis steer for a while and when they got up by the marina Anthony had Francis bring her about. And nobody got clobbered by the boom and nobody had to swim for the centerboard. True, on the return trip Anthony oversailed the dock and they had to use the paddles to row back to it. But all in all, it was a pretty good day to be a pirate. After that day everything changed, mostly.

It turned out the girl cousin was going to be useless for righting the boat. Teresa was smaller than Anthony, but not so young that he had to baby her. So Anthony didn't. Anthony told her how he'd bought Aurora for a dollar. He proudly pointed out his boat, tied up to the dock. Teresa didn't complain that Aurora ought to be taken out of the water and painted. They climbed aboard. She didn't whine that she was going to get wet, or that there was no place clean to sit. Teresa had wild hair that wind and salt water weren't going to ruin. So they sat in the boat, tied up to the dock. And it was OK.

Anthony explained all the cool things about Aurora and Teresa nodded. He showed her how you pull on ropes and make the sails move. He waved his hand about the cove to places he'd sailed and held it up flat and level to show her the height of the waves he'd braved. And Teresa nodded. And it was OK. Until she said what she said.

"You really don't know what you're talking about."

That made so little sense that Anthony stopped talking. It was, after all, his boat.

"Every rope in a sailboat," said Teresa, "has a name. They're called lines. And you have to call every line by its proper name. And the name of none of them is a 'rope'."

This was just stupid. Just like a girl to want fancy names for things that don't need 'em.

"It's my boat. I can call the ropes anything I want," said Anthony, using his captain's voice. Surprisingly, that didn't shut her up.

"Actually, No. You can't. You have to use the proper names."

"It's. My. Boat."

Teresa didn't even pause. "Say you're out on the water and the wind comes about. You tell your crew to pull on that rope over there. You have to free up one hand to point at the 'rope'. Your crew has to stop what he's doing and look back at you to see where you're pointing. And at that point, you're capsized. Captain and crew." She fluffed her hair like all of this was obvious.

Anthony stood up in the boat to tower over her. Aurora rocked. Teresa reached for the gunwales with steadying hands.

"You," said Anthony, turning red. "You. You don't live anywhere near the coast. You've got no right to talk about sailing. I bet you've never sailed in your life."

"Have too."

"Like fun. Don't make me laugh. Where have you sailed? Maybe Kansas?"

"On a lake."

Anthony had her now. "Lake? Ha! That's not real sailing. We sail in the ocean here. Says so on the license plates. Lake," Anthony smirked, "that's kiddie stuff."

"The lake is called Michigan," said Teresa.

Teresa was going to be here for two whole weeks. Anthony made a solemn vow to several saints that he would never untie the rope holding Aurora to the dock while she was still around.

The Tuesday after the Mintons arrived, his mother asked if Teresa and her father could take the boat out for a sail. It was one of those parent questions where you already know what your answer has to be before they stop talking. If you mumble, you're not actually saying yes.

So Teresa took Aurora out. Big deal. She and her father talked about it at dinner afterwards. Anthony's uncle George thanked him for the loan of his boat. He said they had a very pleasant sail. Teresa said the boom vang should be cleated, not just tied off. She said the pocket would be smoother if he was using the Cunningham eyelet. Anthony wasn't listening.

The next day Anthony set up a secret meeting with Francis. They dismounted and walked their bicycles from the hot asphalt to the sandy dirt behind the bait shack where they keep the lobster traps. They leaned the bikes there, well out of sight. Anthony unslung his newsboy delivery bag.

"Look, I got this book on sailing from the library. But I've got to keep it at your house." Anthony balanced the big hardbound book on the saddle of Francis' bike.

Francis hefted *Chapman Piloting and Seamanship*, gripping it by its corners like it was dangerous. "I don't know, my Mom…"

"You gotta do this for me. There's stuff in this book I've got to know. Thing is, I can't let Teresa know that I need to read a book to know it. You have to hide it for me."

Francis tried to pass it back. "Can't you just stash it under your mattress?"

"You have no idea about girl cousins, Francis. They've got like twenty-five eyes in their head. And they ask questions. Like it's everybody's job to answer."

"Well, OK. But I've got to warn you, my Mom has a deathly fear of overdue fines. If she even sees a library book, she takes it back."

"You can do this. You have to. You've hidden stuff from your mom lots of times."

"Yeah, magazines and stuff. But not a whole big hardback book," said Francis. "And if I've got it, how are you going to read it?"

Anthony stiffened and glanced all around, like a girl cousin was sneaking up on them. Between the bait shack and the shore there was nothing but the stack of lobster pots, a junk pile, some scrubby beach roses, and the type of dune grass that scratches up your legs. The back of the bait shack smelled pretty cruddy. And they liked that about it. But that was no guarantee with Teresa. She was weird. She might even show up someplace that smelled bad.

"We just got to do this. And another thing Francis, I almost forgot. You've got to read it too. All of it."

"Me? It's *your* boat."

"Yeah. But you're *my* crew."

Whoever this Chapman guy was, he knew way too much about just about everything. It was like being stuck in a classroom with a history teacher who really actually likes history. After plowing through twenty-five pages or so, Anthony's eyes glazed over, and he gave himself permission to jump around. He'd open *Chapman* at some random spot and read enough to figure out if he needed to know about that. Usually it was something useless, like 'celestial navigation.' So he'd jump somewhere else and read another random page. He'd spend an hour, sometimes two, bouncing around trying to find stuff Teresa wouldn't know. When he was done, he'd move his bookmark ahead maybe fifty pages, then bicycle it back over to Francis.

"I can't believe you're reading all of this boat stuff," said Francis.

"Yep," said Anthony, flicking his bookmark. "Pretty much. It's called seamanship. That's our secret weapon. See, it's got the words 'sea' and 'man' in it. That disqualifies Teresa twice over."

"So we're both learning 'seamanship'?"

"Ok, 'seamenship'."

Francis broke into a goofy grin. "Semen," he said. "Got you to say it."

"Anthony," said his father across the rampart of cereal boxes, "your cousin Teresa is only here for a few more days. You should take her out sailing in your boat."

The spoon froze in the air halfway to his mouth.

"Sure, Dad." Maybe Dad was just saying stuff. Like Dads do. But he didn't stop there.

"I was thinking today, if that's good for the Mintons." Teresa shot a glance at her parents like a cornered animal.

"That's a capital idea!" said Uncle George. Anthony's mom's brother said stuff like that.

"We could pack a picnic, go down to the beach and watch them from there," said Aunt Maeve.

Anthony tried to think fast. "Um, I promised Francis I'd do something with him. Something important. All day."

"I don't see how that could be," said his mother. "I talked to Gail just yesterday and she said she was taking Francis school shopping."

He threw Teresa the silent universal kid signal of "help me out here." Teresa just gazed into the well of her cereal bowl, like she was contemplating her own reflection, or maybe death by drowning.

Though Mom had just sold him out, she was still his best bet. "Um, Teresa isn't used to tides. I mean, a lake isn't salt water, so they don't have tides. It's going to be wicked low today and that's, you know, *dangerous*."

Teresa looked up from her Cheerios. "First of all," she said "tides have *nothing* to do with whether the water is salty. They have to do with the moon. We do too have tides on Lake Michigan, twice a day just like here. Though our waves are significantly more choppy, and we get more frequent wind shifts," said Miss Know-it-all. "Sailing here is actually pretty easy."

Easy? How was that supposed to help? Don't girls know anything about lying?

"Then it's settled. We'll pack a lunch and see you off at the dock."

He knew it was futile, but he had to try "Dad, a girl on a boat? That's. That's."

"It's *what*?" said Teresa.

"Nothing," Anthony mumbled into his breakfast bowl, a single Cheerio adrift like an abandoned life buoy.

The whole extended family came down to the dock to see them off. They even packed them a lunch, like the two cousins were going to sit out there in the middle of the cove and unwrap waxed paper sandwiches. Anthony took the captain's seat by the tiller. He ordered Teresa to untie the *painter*. Teresa said "casting off." They pushed Aurora backwards until she cleared the dock. He told her to pull on the front *halyard*. She said "raising the jib." They caught the wind. A nice easy offshore wind turned them into open water, and their parents called after them "good luck." Right.

And, surprisingly, it was OK. At least Teresa knew who was captain, and she did what he told her to do. He held the tiller and told her which way they were going to sail. She raised the mainsail and he moved it back and forth with the boom ropes. *Sheets.* Dumbest name ever. She handled the jib. The rest of what she was doing he did his best to ignore.

She kept saying stuff about 'reaches' which made no sense. She could easily reach anything she needed to pull on. And she kept messing with the centerboard. Everybody knows the centerboard is just there to keep the wind from knocking your boat over. And if it did, at least with Francis they could put enough weight on it to get Aurora back upright. Anthony wasn't so sure with skinny Teresa. But she kept pulling it up. Was Lake Michigan that shallow? And what if she had the stupid centerboard up and the wind dunked them over? What were they going to stand on then?

Anthony tried to stay above it all. The sailing was what mattered, right? If he could ignore Francis' complaining, he could ignore Teresa's fussing with things and explaining. He leaned back in his captain's seat, took a deep breath of sea air, and looked up at his Aurora's beautiful white wings. And then he saw it.

"What the hell is that?" he said, pointing to a *pink hair ribbon* fluttering from his mainsail.

"We're not supposed to say 'hell'. It's like taking the Lord's Name in vain. Only backwards."

He could ignore Teresa, but she had no right to ignore him. That was mutiny. Anthony pointed at the thing with his whole arm, as if she didn't already know what he was talking about. It wasn't any of those lines whose names he had memorized from *Chapman*. It wasn't a rope at all. It was *definitely* a ribbon.

"I'll say a lot worse than 'hell'. What is it? And what's it doing on My Boat?"

"It's a tell-tale," said Teresa, like that settled everything.

"It's *pink*."

"It tells you how closely to trim so you don't end up luffing."

"Whatever that's supposed to mean, I don't want it on My Boat," said Anthony. "Take it down. Now!"

Teresa gazed up at the rippling sails, like decorating Aurora with ribbons was a 'capital idea'. "Strike the mainsail? In this wind?"

"Take that God-damn ponytail ribbon off my boat. Now."

Teresa started to say 'We're not supposed to say…', but stopped herself. Instead, she said, "You're the captain. Dropping the main."

Aurora heeled suddenly when Teresa let the mainsail go. The loose canvas snapped angrily in the wind as his crew struggled to bring it under control. Anthony pushed the tiller hard to keep them from capsizing.

There was a scraping noise along the bottom of the boat. Then Aurora stopped abruptly, dead in the water.

"What the…"

"I don't know. You're the captain." The tell-tale gave a final flutter as Teresa finished securing the mainsail.

"Yeah, but. What just happened?" Anthony looked around but there was nothing but salt water from here to the shore.

Teresa leaned over the left side of the boat. Anthony was pretty sure that was called the *port* side.

She stared into the water for a long time like she was admiring her reflection.

"We sailed over a mooring buoy," she finally reported.

"So?"

"Apparently, we're moored."

"What?"

"We're snagged on the mooring."

That makes no sense, thought Anthony. A buoy is just, like, a buoy. It's just floating there.

"It looks like we sailed between the mooring buoy and the pick-up. The actual mooring is big and heavy, so they've got a little pick-up buoy to gaff in. They're tied together."

"So we're snagged on that *line*?"

"Actually, *that* is called a *rope*. The pick-up rope is wedged between our stern and our rudder. It was an easy target, since you had it sideways, hard to port, when we struck. Now it's wedged that way. Go ahead, try it."

Anthony gave the sideways tiller a yank. It moved about an inch, then bounced back. He looked over the stern down into the water and saw a murky orange nylon rope stuck like dental floss just where Teresa said it would be.

This isn't supposed to happen, thought Anthony. This is the kind of bad luck you get when the priest says *bodyofChrist* and hands you the Eucharist. And you drop it. Not that Anthony had ever fumbled the communion wafer, but he had imagined it happening every single Sunday. That kind of bad luck. And it was her fault.

"It's your fault," he said.

Teresa busied herself lowering the jib. With her back to Anthony, she said with a kind of terrible calm. "My fault? I can think of at least twelve ways that this is, in fact, your fault," she paused, "captain."

Anthony was pretty sure he could swim to shore. Leave his stupid cousin stuck out here. Serve her right. She'd be marooned until whoever owned this damn mooring came back to find her.

But a captain never abandons his ship. And then there's parents. No matter what dumb thing your visiting cousin does, your parents expect you to look out for them, to not abandon them. He had the best excuse in the world. But Anthony knew his parents wouldn't hear it.

"Do you have a screwdriver?"

He was trying to think, and she was, as usual, asking questions.

"If we had a screwdriver, we could unship the rudder and free the pick-up rope. In a *normal* boat you'd just pull the rudder pintles out of the gudgeons, but this one has its rudder screwed down with great big door hinges."

Anthony remembered how proud he was when he screwed those hardware store hinges into the stern. That rudder wasn't going anywhere this time.

"That makes it thirteen ways," said Teresa. "So, do you have one?"

"Nope."

"How about a knife? Do you have a rigging knife?"

"Go Fish."

Teresa was quiet for a while. She went up to the bow and fiddled with something up there. Then she came back past the mast to Anthony. "Do you want a sandwich?" she said, holding out a wax-paper baggie to him.

As they were finishing their sandwiches, Anthony spotted some sailboats in the distance approaching them. "Hey! Here come some boats. If we get their attention maybe they'll stop and help us out. I bet one of them has a gudgeon, or whatever it was you said we needed."

"They're not going to stop for us," said Teresa, "that's a regatta."

"Listen, I don't know how stuck-up Italians are in Michigan, but here in Rhode Island they're wicked friendly. Dollars to donuts they'd help a couple of kids out of a jam. All we have to do is flag them down."

Anthony started waving his arms overhead. Teresa didn't join in. She just watched the sailboats in silence. "Anthony, a regatta isn't an Italian sailboat. It's a sailboat race. That's why they're not going to stop."

"People race sailboats?"

"That's what sailboats are *for*," said Teresa. "Watch what they're doing. They've rounded the first mark and those two are bearing off. Number 16 is overtaking the 22 to windward. 16 is shadowing him, stealing his air. He's making his move. There. He's rolled him, taking the lead. So the 22 has got to overlap him before the 16 can jibe across his bow. But look way over there: the number 11 rounded, then it looks like he's heading off course. Not a chance. He's on a jibe set into clean air. Now he makes his second jibe, well to leeward. He's found the breeze and is picking up speed on a broad reach. Coming on strong. The other two are running downwind, but the 11 is going to force them to go after his wind. The 22 is to the leeward of 16, and the overlap prevents the 16 from jibing. There goes 22 – jibe-ho! – retaking the lead. 16 is hurting. He's chasing 22 but now he's forced to jibe into dirty air to leeward. And that tricky 11 doesn't have to change course, so he's now in contention."

Anthony wasn't listening. He was watching, rapt. People race sailboats.

Once the regatta disappeared into the distance, Anthony's brain returned to their circumstances. "It looks like one of us is going to have to swim," said Anthony. He stripped off his shirt. "I'm the captain."

He dove off the stern. Treading water, he tried to pull the pick-up buoy loose. It was wedged tight and wouldn't budge. He took a deep breath, dove underwater and yanked at the nylon rope. It was slick in his hands and he couldn't get enough of a grip to loosen it where it was pinched against the flat of the rudder blade. He rose to the surface and gasped another lungful of air. He dove again, looping the rope around his hand. That helped, but he still wasn't getting anywhere. He just didn't have anything to press against. He was just floating out there, yanking on a slimy orange rope. He tried holding onto the mooring chain, but that only left him one hand to work at the jammed buoy rope. And Aurora had a mind of her own and kept drifting away from the mooring. That wasn't going to work either.

He surfaced for the fifth or sixth time and there was Teresa, leaning over the stern, supervising.

"You don't have enough leverage," she said.

Cold, wet, and frustrated, Anthony was composing an apt reply.

"I'm going to lower the centerboard," she continued, "once it's down you can swim under the boat and brace your feet against it."

"That might actually work," conceded Anthony. And it did.

Back on dry land. Back at the dinner table. Uncle George asked how the sailing went.

"Uneventful," said Teresa. "It was a good day on the water."

"Capital," said Uncle George.

Anthony shot her a secret smile and nodded.

Some kids get driven to piano lessons. Some kids get driven to Little League. Anthony got driven to sailing school. The main difference is that ballet lessons don't start with being deliberately capsized into cold salty water.

Not that Anthony thought he needed to go to sailing school. OK, there were a few things he still didn't get, but how important could they be? Just some Teresa technicalities. But when he tried to sign

Aurora up for the Youth Regatta at the East Bay Sailing Club he ran aground on the question 'Sailing School or Water Safety Certification?' So he was going to Sailing School.

For reasons that made no sense to him, Anthony had to learn how to sail in a boat he wouldn't be caught dead sailing in. He already had a boat, but Aurora was left tethered to the dock while Anthony attempted to stay afloat in a one-hander the size of a Dixie Cup.

At least Anthony knew a few things. Thanks to Teresa, he knew the proper names of every bit of rigging on a real sailboat. That gave him some points with Mr. D., the sailing instructor. And he knew that these clown cars weren't real sailboats because he owned a real sailboat. He also knew that St. Nicholas is the patron saint of sailors, students, and children. Not bad for Santa Claus. That gave him someone to ask for help.

The first three lessons on the water, Anthony blamed the idiotic tiny sailboat for everything that went wrong. After all, Anthony already knew how to sail, so why was everything going sideways? By the fourth lesson, he added the constantly shouting instructor to the list of culprits. When wind, waves, and tides were added to the guilty parties, Anthony finally had to admit that he had something to learn.

He learned that you can't let the wind tell you where you're going. You read the wind, then use it to go in whatever direction you want. Points of sail. Seems pretty obvious when you're looking at posters where the wind is a great big arrow and your puny boat is a neat little outline. Not so obvious when you can't see it, it's pushing you around in gusty puffs out there and waves are slapping you broadside.

If you're not capsizing, you're not learning. That was Mr. D.'s official rule of sailing school. "I will make you fisher-outers of men." Mr. D.'s other rule wasn't spoken but was known by all: If you're colliding you're going to get yelled at, even when it's not your fault. There was lots of water out there. But it seemed like those seven dinky little boats insisted on bumper cars with each other every chance they got. And the only way to avoid collisions was to do something abrupt and heroic. And that capsized you. One other thing you quickly learned was to keep at least one boat between yourself and Number 4. Jeez, some people should just stay on land.

Sitting in Aurora at the dock he read from his notebook to her what he had learned in sailing school. There was no one else to tell. Francis was nowhere to be found. Teresa had returned to the Midwest and was no doubt sailing back and forth from one bank of Lake Michigan to the other. He wanted to write his cousin, but he didn't know how to do it like it was no big deal. If she wrote him, then he could write back. That was just good manners. But how could he start writing? And would he tell her he was in Sailing School, like he needed to be in Sailing School? No way. He flipped through his spiral notebook, reading aloud to Aurora all the points boxing the compass. Not that she needed to know that. "South-southwest a quarter west. That's Block Island."

But if Teresa would write to him. Like a thank you note for taking her out sailing. Not much chance of that. "In irons: straight into the wind; avoid, no way to sail it," he read aloud. Teresa would just make fun of him, in her superior way. "On the hard: a boat out of the water." But Anthony could ask her about her boat, which was Uncle George's boat. Then he could remind her that Aurora was his own boat. His boat. But she would have to write to him first.

Anthony tore a blank page out of the spiral notebook. He started folding it. He folded a perfect little sailboat. He could send that to Teresa. She would have to write back.

At the end of sailing school, Mr. D. announced that the next week they would have a race. A short course from the starting line around a buoy and back again. After weeks of tack and jibe, this perked Anthony's interest.

"For the race, we will re-assign the school boats. You've gotten too comfortable with the one you've been sailing. In a new boat you'll have to depend on your skills."

Comfortable? Does that mean bobbing around in a plastic bathtub? Of course, Anthony would be switching to a different boat. Her name is Aurora. Too bad most of these kids don't have boats of their own for the big race.

"I don't need one of these practice boats. I'm going to bring Aurora."

"Aurora is your boat?"

Anthony nodded.

"Sorry Anthony. You can't. You can only race with your own class."

"But I would be racing with my class. That's what you just said."

"No, not the sailing class. The class of boat. Aurora can only race against boats in her own class."

"She's a sailboat, a sailing dinghy. Just not a dinky dinghy."

"Yes, but what class of sailing dinghy?"

"First Class? Catechism class? Beats me."

Mr. D. explained that all sailboats belong to a class according to who designed them, and often what version of that design. Boat designers are legendary. Every good sailor knows who designed his boat. There's a letter or a logo on the mainsail that says what design she is.

Aurora didn't come with a mainsail. His Dad got one that kinda fits (it's a little short for the mast), but it doesn't say anything. Anthony hadn't seen the guy with the crewcut since he sold her to him, but he was pretty sure he wouldn't want to answer questions.

"I'm assigning you boat Number 4 for the race."

Number 4. The worst sailor in every class exercise. But then Anthony had the scary thought that maybe it wasn't that the kid in Number 4 was a terrible sailor. Maybe it was the boat. Maybe the Number 4 boat was cursed. Say somebody died in it, or something. That happens.

"Perhaps tomorrow I'll come and take a look at Aurora. I'm sure we can figure out what class she is. Today let's focus on the race."

Anthony was excited to finally be in a sailboat race, though not in this plastic boat or with these competitors. Most of them had never sailed before and, judging by their abilities, a couple of them would probably never sail again. The race turned out to be as big a mess as Anthony feared, except for the part about the curse. The #4 boat did about as well as he could expect from a toy boat.

Mr. D. stood up in a little motorboat at the starting line and blew the air horn. But the #5 boat was already over the starting line, so she had to turn around and go back to the line. Jibe. Since everyone else was moving forward while she was making a U turn, half of the boats were tangled up at the starting line and never really recovered. Only Anthony and two other boats made a clean start. Everyone forgot the most basic rules. Even Rule 10: *When boats are on opposite tacks, a port-tack boat shall keep clear of a starboard-tack boat*. They acted like "keeping clear" meant just not crashing into each other. Can't wait until these guys get drivers licenses. Anthony was on the starboard tack; fat lot of good it did him, he still had to veer from his course or hear the grinding sounds of plastic on plastic, immediately followed by Mr. D.'s yelling. That is, if Mr. D. had actually been watching, rather than motoring around in a circle trying to sort out the starting boats. Number 2 should have taken a penalty. Anthony penalized him all right. As they came on the buoy, Anthony overtook and passed him on the windward side, stealing his air and leaving him luffing too close to the wind to tack out of it. After that it was just jibe-ho and a run downwind against the #7 boat who couldn't tell a mainsail from a burlap bag of wind. Across the line and home. Anthony had won his first race. It was a victory, but not much of a triumph. In his next race he'd show some real sailors what he and Aurora could do.

The following afternoon Anthony biked over to the dock and sat swinging his legs, watching fingerlings dodging around the pilings. As promised, Mr. D. drove out there to look Aurora over. Mr. D. took a quick look at Aurora. Then a longer look. He walked out to the end of the dock and stood there staring at her bow. He chewed on his knuckle, then went back to his truck, pulled open the passenger side door and got a big book and a ditty bag containing a camera, notebook, tape measure, and a clanking collection of other stuff. He climbed aboard Aurora and stretched the tape measure this way and that, scratched his head, paged through his big boat encyclopedia, and wrote down some more measurements.

Anthony knew not to interrupt adults. But his fidgeting spoke volumes. Finally, Mr. D. answered the question.

"As near as I can tell, she's not in any class. She's what's known as a basement boat. Built by the original owner," said Mr. D. "And not from a kit."

"Is that a bad thing?" said Anthony.

But Mr. D. didn't respond. He was somewhere far away where adults go for no reason. "Beautiful lines."

They looked like ordinary ropes to Anthony, but boat people are weird that way.

"Look at the cut of her bow, the sheer of the transom," continued Mr. D., though it wasn't clear he was talking to Anthony. "Whoever built you was *someone*. This can't be a one-off. His signature has to be here somewhere, some design detail I just haven't noticed." Mr. D. ran his hand along the gunwale like he was stroking a cat. "I wish we had the original sails," he sighed. Then Mr. D. just sat there in Anthony's boat for the longest time.

"Excuse me but," said Anthony. "If Aurora isn't in any class, then she's in a class by herself? That's supposed to be special, right? I always knew she was special. So, can I race her?"

"No." said Mr. D. "I mean, technically yes. But still mostly no." Mr. D. put away his tape measure and stepped up onto the dock. He pulled a battered camera from the ditty bag and photographed Aurora from every angle he could think of, winding the film forward between clicks until the winder stopped dead at the end of the roll. His "no" hung in the air like a seasick smell.

Finally, Mr. D. continued: "Have you ever heard of a sea lawyer? Sailboat racing is full of them. They argue about everything. Race committees for decades have been creating ever more elaborate formulas to level the playing field. It's the waterline ratio of this to the square root of the sail area of that. You need an advanced degree in mathematics to know if your boat even qualifies. And for decades boat designers have been twisting boats into pretzels to meet, undermine, and circumvent those formulas," said Mr. D. "For the better part of a century a 12 Metre boat has actually had no measurement on it that's 12 meters.

"That's the tragedy of boat design. It's like cramming to pass a standardized test and calling that wisdom. Whoever built Aurora wasn't trying to cheat their way into the club. He was simply building something beautiful, a harmony of wood and water and wind. So no, you can't race her."

Like much of what adults say, Anthony figured he didn't need to understand most of this. "You said 'technically yes'."

"Right. First-across-the-finish-line racing is out of the question. But the damn sea lawyers have come up with a system for handicapping dissimilar boats. PHRF. The P is for Performance, the H is for Heaven help you."

"So Aurora has to handicap the other boats? Do I give them a head start?"

"Worse than that. You race and cross the finish line third or fourth. Then a team of sea lawyers and saltwater mathematicians argue out whether or not you actually won the race. You can imagine how the other boats feel about this."

"That doesn't sound like much fun."

"My feelings exactly."

Anthony tried to think of a way around it, but it was the kind of thing that adults do, filling every inch of fun with a hundred pounds of rules. Cousin Teresa said that racing is what sailboats are *for*. Mr. D. told him that Aurora was even better than Anthony had always felt her to be. She was made to go faster than anything. And now nobody would let her into a race.

Mr. D. must have seen Anthony's face, because he tried to offer some glimmer of hope. "There's one other possibility. Whoever built Aurora spent a huge amount of time making the complex and precise jig required to shape her curves. No sane boatwright would go to all that effort to build only one boat. It just doesn't make any sense. So somewhere out there it's likely that she has sisters. A whole new class of sailboats. We just have no idea where to look."

Mr. D. looked up and down the cove, as if more boats would appear like birds in a flock.

"Who was the man who sold Aurora to your parents?"

"He didn't sell it to my *parents*. He sold Aurora to me. For a dollar. She's my boat. Hundred percent," said Anthony.

"So who was he? Man who sold her?"

"Dunno what his name was. He wanted to burn her, but the Fire Department wouldn't let him."

"There is a God," said Mr. D.

That evening Anthony received a letter from Michigan. Ignoring his mother's question, he rushed it upstairs where he could open it in private. The envelope from Teresa felt kind of lumpy; when he ripped it open a paper sailboat fell out onto his desk. She had sent him a letter folded into a sailboat. Cool.

No. She had sent him *his* sailboat. Not cool. Cold. Sent it back to him. Like she didn't want it. Anthony searched the empty envelope for some kind of note. Nothing. He balled up the envelope, stepped back the regulation distance and set-shot into the trash can. His stupid paper boat. Mailed it to her so she'd have to write back. Lamest idea ever. Anthony was about to crumple it when he noticed a thin line of letters running around the inside edge of the hull.

"*Double ender. Bermuda rigged. Needed a daggerboard, so I added one.*"

And indeed, there was a slot scissored in the bottom of the hull and a little slip of paper inserted. Anthony pushed down on the daggerboard and it poked out below the origami boat. There was a note in precise tiny letters written on it.

"*Nice boat, but I prefer Aurora. How is she? If she is good, I know you are too. Write back. T.*"

Autumn was cold, blustery, and wet. Leaves congealed into soggy lumps blocking the rip currents along the gutters, whirling new-fallen maple sailors into eddies. Middle School, that immense distraction, filled more and more of the view as day followed day and the teachers, seeing the wind go out of their classes, consigned their students to rowing through the textbooks.

Francis had discovered Pop Warner Football and had to schedule weekend sailing around his scrimmage practice. Being Francis, from the moment they left the dock he complained about the cold water, even though they no longer turned turtle like they had in their pirate days. The skills learned in sailing school gave Anthony a more confident hand, and Aurora responded to it enthusiastically. When they ran with the wind even Francis forgot the cold and whooped at their newfound speed. But he crewed with one eye glancing back toward the dock, worried that too much fun would take them too far and he would be last on the field and have to count pushups for his transgression.

Running down the wind or beating against it, no distance or chill salty spray could dampen Anthony's spirit. Sailing was better than life. Once on the water his only unfulfilled wish was that Francis' wristwatch would cease to be waterproof and time would stop. He'd have to confess that to the priest and take his Hail Marys.

Every other sailboat off her mooring was the subject of an implicit race. Usually, the Sunday sailors gave way or ignored Aurora completely. But occasionally one gave chase, and that was a good day.

Sailing back to shore, they saw the glint of binoculars. As they approached, the figures on the dock resolved into Anthony's father and Mr. D. standing together waiting there for them. No sooner was painter tied to piling than Francis was sprinting for his bicycle, late again, grabbing up his white football helmet from the saddle and strapping it on like some motorcycle daredevil.

"Anthony, I need to speak to you about something," said his father.

The boy glanced from his dad to Mr. D. and back again, trying to anticipate what was about to happen.

"Mr. D'Ambrosio has been doing some research on our boat and he's found out something significant."

Our? "Dad, Aurora is my boat. Remember? You had to sign because I was underaged. But it was my dollar. She's my boat."

"I'm afraid she's our boat," said his father. "You're still underaged. I have legal liability."

Dad was taking Aurora away from him. That's what adults do, they let kids have stuff. But then they take it away whenever they feel like it. They ground you, they take away what they call "your privileges" any time you break one of their rules. They throw out stuff because they've decided you should have outgrown it. And they take your boat when they find out it's a better boat than they thought it was.

Mr. D. spoke up. "Anthony, when I got the photos of Aurora back from the drug store, I noticed something. Something that told me where she came from." Anthony had looked everywhere. Nobody had carved their name into the wood to say 'This boat belongs to'. Heck, kids carve their names into school desks in classes that they don't even like. He was at that moment sorry that he hadn't carved at least his initials, with Mr. D. and his father on the dock implying that Aurora wasn't his after all.

"Did the guy put his name on her somewhere, maybe in some secret boatbuilder's code?" said Anthony.

"No," said Mr. D., "nothing like that. What I noticed is that the rudder is attached with old door hinges."

"Yeah. That." Anthony mumbled. "That was kind of my mistake." Cousin Teresa had already given him grief about it. Could they take Aurora away from him for using the wrong hinges?

"A proper sailboat…"

"I know. Uses grudges and pintles."

"Gudgeons," corrected Mr. D. "I figured you put the hinges on. What I noticed in the photo was that there weren't any marks in the wood where the original gudgeons went. Anthony, when you found Aurora the rudder wasn't attached, was it?"

"It was just lying in the bottom of the boat, half-buried in sand. It was the only thing in the boat. I had to find that hockey stick handle to make a tiller. I got the hinges," admitted Anthony, "from the junk pile behind the bait shop."

"It's amazing the rudder was still there, given the circumstances."

The only circumstances Anthony remembered was a boat stranded far up on the beach and an angry man kicking her.

"What the photograph told me," said Mr. D. "was that the rudder had never been attached. You can't sail a boat without a rudder. So that means you were the first to ever sail Aurora."

Somehow, Anthony had always known that. He loved Aurora. Aurora loved him back. The guy with the crewcut who sold her for a dollar had never loved

Aurora. He had never sailed in Aurora. He couldn't have.

"When you build a sailboat, the rudder is just about the last thing you attach. But there were no gudgeons. Aurora was an unfinished boat. The boatbuilder never completed the project. And that explains a lot."

2

Carol Vandermann, 1954

There was a storm coming up the coast with her name on it. She couldn't help but take it personally. Adding insult to injury.

There was nothing wrong with the old system, using good old military names for the big storms: alpha, bravo, charlie, delta. Then some wag decided that they would start using women's names for hurricanes. It was about as stupid a male thing as she could think of, but it made perfect guy sense: if something that unpredictable and furious was going to happen, a woman had to be to blame.

It was August and both of her children were home from school. At least that was something. Melissa was in the house, and Greg, the eldest, had walked over to the Catholic church to buy some candles. Carol knew that you weren't supposed to take the candles away with you. You were supposed to leave them in the rack to warm Mary's outstretched hands. But plumbers candles were about the first thing that had sold out in the stores. And the Vandermanns weren't Catholic, so she viewed the whole Mary statuary thing with some suspicion.

Their house was well inland. That again was something. It had a big basement to accommodate the coal chute with its spilled pile of last winter's leftover heat next to the cold crouching iron boiler. As the hurricane approached, the basement accommodated a radio with big cannister batteries, cot beds, and jerry cans of water. Steven was a planner. No storm would catch him off guard, even one with his wife's name attached to it.

Of course, if Steven had his way, their house would be as close to Narragansett Bay as he could manage. The Bay was his life and his livelihood, and every moment spent inland seemed somehow stolen from that great basin of salt water. The compromise was that Carol would have a home with zinnias and respectable neighbors and a good school system, and Steven could have his workshop down with the vagrant clammers and the scalloping boats on the coast.

In every year of their 20-year marriage Steven would reassure Carol that this was going to be the breakthrough year. It was, some years more than others. His Integrated Wheelhouse design made that part of a working boat not just some add-on that could be swept off the deck. A wave would as soon sink a trawler as uproot the substructure of Steven's sturdy enclosure. The sale of the patents had bankrolled their new Chrysler Imperial with the revolutionary Ausco-Lambert 4-wheel disc braking system. Other years they made do on whatever nautical repairs and maintenance Steven could scrape together.

The sky was turning ugly and the Chrysler was nowhere in sight. Greg was back with the candles, and now Melissa wanted to go out to fill up the bird feeder. The poor birds had to be out in bad weather, she reasoned, and they were going to be wet and hungry.

Carol's phone rang like an alarm. Greg picked up and handed it to her with the comment "It's Dad."

Dad was still at the boatyard. He had just finished boarding up the windows on the boatbuilder's shed. He joked that he was going to paint 'Carol Go Away' on the barricades. There was static on the line. She pressed the black handset to her ear and spiraled the coiled cord nervously about a finger. Steven's voice was distant but he sounded calm. She could hear him pacing around the workshop as far as the phone wire would reach, fidgeting with his free hand. She knew him well enough to know that his attention was engaged where he was and that nothing she said would arrive at the other end of the line. So she listened in the handset to wind howling in circles around the boat shed. She listened to the faint sounds of Steven's tacking hammer. More static. "And then I need to batten down this year's Breakthrough." Another scheme to make his fortune. The whole family had been hearing about Her every day for at least a year and a half. "Off the jigs. But still on the hard." Steven was nearly finished with the prototype for a new class of small sailboats he called 'Auroras,' named after the goddess of the new dawn.

She heard the phone set down on the table. She heard the mingled sounds of wind and water. And the report of hammering further away across the room. And the voice of Steven, alone in the boat-building shed, talking soothingly to something in cadences that sounded like prayer.

That was the last any of them heard from Steven.

"Once we realized that Aurora was an unfinished boat, we stopped looking for boats and started looking for boatyards. Or places where boatyards used to be," said Mr. D. "You're probably too young to remember it, but Hurricane Carol pretty much wiped out the boatbuilding industry here."

Anthony was not too young to remember the sound of the storm, a roar that rose and rose and never stopped. Or the bright sunshine afterwards. Or his favorite climbing tree lying uprooted in the front yard.

"I think he remembers, Mike," said Anthony's father.

"Sorry," said Mr. D. "Anyway, it appears that the boatbuilder attempted to ride out the storm at his boatyard…"

"So the man with the crewcut who sold Aurora to me?"

"That was the boatwright's son. Greg."

"And that's where the problem is, Anthony," said his father. "Four years later the town was trying to clean up the last of the derelicts from the big storm. Somehow, they found the Vandermanns. Greg was supposed to move Aurora off town property. It wasn't a labor of love. He didn't want her. But he wasn't authorized to sell her. He couldn't."

"But I bought her. He signed a paper. I gave him a dollar."

"'Signed' is an overstatement," said Mr. D. "Greg's signature was illegible. The town was no help. So it took some time. Asking around at wharfs up and down the coast with my photos."

"The sale wasn't valid," continued his father. "Greg Vandermann didn't own her so he couldn't sell her."

"Then who…?" said Anthony.

"Greg's mother. Carol Vandermann. The widow of the boat designer. And she believes with all her heart that Aurora killed her husband."

"Killed?" said Anthony.

"She says that her husband had made provisions to shelter from Hurricane Carol with the family inland, but that he was so preoccupied with protecting the boat he was building that he never left the boat-house. Carol of '54 was a huge storm. Like nothing anyone had seen before. A direct hit on Rhode Island. Not a stick of the boatbuilding shed remained, but Steven Vandermann's car was found parked next to the foundation slab. It was filled to the window trim with salt water.

"Hurricane Carol lifted Aurora off the boatshed rack and dumped her in the cove, far up on the beach, high and dry, but by some miracle unharmed. Or maybe not a miracle, maybe just a really well-made sailboat."

"But that guy was trying to kick Aurora apart."

"And he wasn't able to. Though it was within his rights to try. What he couldn't do was sell her."

"Dad? Can we buy Aurora all over again? Buy her from the mom? Please?"

"I don't know, son. I don't think she wants to sell."

Dear Cousin Teresa,

How are you? I am fine. It turns out the guy who built Aurora is dead. So I am not fine. He mostly built her, but just before he was finished he was killed by Carol. Not his wife Carol, the hurricane named Carol. So Carol (the wife) thinks Aurora has a curse. But Aurora is my boat and she doesn't have a curse. Except she's not my boat any more. Even though I'm the only one who ever sailed her. Except for you and Uncle George. You also sailed her. And you and I sailed her. OK, we snagged on a mooring buoy. But that's not a deadman's curse. I don't think she's cursed, do you? Please write ASAP, because I need to buy her back.

Anthony

Dear Cousin Anthony,

Yes, having someone die in a boatbuilding accident can definitely curse a boat. That's what happened to the Charles Haskell. Boatyard worker fell from her just before she was launched. Broke his neck. Everyone knew the Haskell was cursed but didn't know how. Turned out the curse started when she rammed and sank another fishing boat in a storm. After that, the ghosts of the drowned fishermen kept coming aboard the Haskell to fish alongside the living ones. As curses go, it's all kind of mixed up, because it seems to me that the boat that got accidentally sunk was even more cursed than the boat that got invaded by her ghosts. I don't think anything that creepy has happened on Aurora, though it's a good thing you didn't try to change her name. Try Holy Water. That usually works.

It sounds like your real problem is that Carol feels cursed by the Aurora, because she misses her husband. Aurora is a beautiful sailboat and maybe that reminds her of how beautiful her husband was, and that hurts. Or maybe she's just mad at him. You have to offer her something she needs. I don't think it's a dollar.

Teresa

Carol Vandermann, 1958

He left us high and dry, in the most literal of senses. Everything Steven had, he put into boats. His time, his money, his attention that was owed us as a family was poured back into the boatyard. His latest baby. Aurora, his girl.

Those of us who are not sailors end up widows. Landlocked and staring from rooftop to horizon for the glimpse of a sail. The ones we would hold are held in thrall elsewhere. A waterborne existence that for the rest of us, mere passengers, is half tedium and half nausea. Seasick, we see them burning with sea fever and cannot fathom the cause. In youthful love this is the sailor's charm. But marriage to a mariner scours off the poetry.

Is there any inanimate object on Earth more adored than a sailboat? Inanimate did I say? Sailors will insist that their sailboat is anything but. That it has a personality, its likes and dislikes. That it must be wooed. Every moment of sweet accord is won by coaxing from a thing willful, peevish, and stubborn. Boats have their quirks and are somehow more beloved for them. They are beautiful. A little vain. And no two are the same.

No sailor would admit that his sailboat was manufactured. A sailboat is always "built". It is a unique creation, a pure expression, even when they know that this cannot possibly be the truth.

A sailing boat exists between sea and sky. As Steven explained it, to build a better boat is to perfect the half in water and the half in wind. And you can't do both. They are contradictory. The wind drives you forward, the seawater holds you back. More sail means more counterbalancing keel, more hull in the water.

The boatwright strives for an impossibility, a hull so contoured and so smooth that the water sheers off it without any turbulence to arrest her progress. Irregularities that the hand cannot sense on the surface of the hull are detected by the water passing over it, setting up eddies that multiply along her length, slowing her down.

Instead, eddies multiplied along the length of our marriage. And then he was gone.

To achieve the perfect smoothness of the hull Steven suspended Aurora in a frame and rack just out of the water's reach. Nothing would ever press against that fine sanded wood and marine varnish except salt water. Her very weight out of water would dent her. When I saw Aurora suspended on high and Steven crouching beneath, my first thought was: Dear God, that boat is going to come crashing down and crush him. Perhaps that is what happened. Or perhaps as the storm heightened Steven felt the boat breaking loose from the rack and threw himself aboard. Something he would do.

It took three years for the towns along the Bay to sort out the unclaimed and derelict boats thrown up upon the coast. Three towns away, Aurora was locally famous, even written up in the ProJo as the mysterious Storm Orphan. Not that we saw it or had any suspicion that Hurricane Carol had reserved for us any further grief after the recovery and funeral of Steven's battered body.

But as if to mock us, that town up the Bay finally attributed Aurora and insisted that we assume responsibility. Or face consequences.

It was as pointlessly painful as stumbling upon a cache of love letters written to someone else. I had no desire to see the ruins of what had ruined us. I sent Greg to take care of it. The rest you know.

Now I realize Greg wasn't the best person to send. Understandably, he hated the boat on sight. He assumed that it was a wreck beyond repair and figured the kid he sold it to would play pirates for a week or two on the dunes. When he lost interest, the flotsam removal would fall on someone else's shoulders, not ours.

Except. Last week we were approached by the manager of the local yacht club with handfuls of photos of Aurora floating at a dock. You could say that this Mike D'Ambrosio was floating himself. He wanted to know everything about Steven and went on and on about Aurora in glowing terms. Not that I understood much of it. But according to this D'Ambrosio, Steven was a boatbuilding genius and Steven's boat is still afloat because it was designed to be indestructible. And D'Ambrosio wanted the rights to copy the design.

And so Aurora has come back from the grave to haunt us. Having gone through the empty birthdays and the family holidays without the head of the household, I thought we had passed through the worst of the grief. But the murder weapon has washed ashore.

"Couldn't you tell the boat wasn't a wreck?"

Greg shrugged. He's my loveable lump of a boy. And when he makes that half-embarrassed grin, it's Steven all over. People try to avoid talking about a death to a widow, not realizing that the death is everywhere. Sometimes I want to shout to my too-careful friends "that's Steven!" Point all around the room at everything he made or fixed or touched. "And that's Steven! And that over there is him too!"

And the last thing he touched is still out there. Floating at a dock, some kid's toy. And so the water is no longer blank. Now every glance at the bay I will be looking for that sail, Steven's shape on the water.

"Mom, I'm wicked sorry. Honest. I didn't know Dad's boat was worth real money."

Whether we were flush enough to buy that dream of a car, or at the grocery store it was day old and dented, it was never about the money. Your husband isn't the breadwinner, he's the bread. Your marriage is nourished by his comings and goings, on his attending to that half of everything that you simply don't notice, on his dear daily oblivion to half of the things you do. Between us we took care of the whole of our lives. That's where the magic lies. How at any moment we could surprise each other with the most obvious things, hidden in plain sight.

Alone, you're broken open like half a fortune cookie.

And floating out there on the bay you catch a distant glimpse of your other half.

"Did that Mr. D'Ambrosio say how much Aurora was worth?" Something to say.

"He made it sound like the sky's the limit. He makes it sound like Dad made some kind of perfect dinghy. I hope he isn't figuring we've got cash to invest, right?"

"One thing your father taught me. There is no perfect boat. There's only a better boat."

"Yeah, but. Those yacht club types would pay plenty for better. We've got to get Dad's boat back."

"I don't know," I said to Greg. And I honestly didn't. If Aurora is our legacy, is it a gift or a curse? Either way, it takes us back into a past we can't make peace with.

"Like I mean, it's not like I really sold it."

"He gave you a dollar. You signed a paper."

"Yeah." said Greg, and he went silent. But I could tell he was still thinking. "But. Could I sell it? Y'know? Maybe only you could sell it, the boat? A next-of-kin kind of thing?"

Dear Teresa,

How are you? I am fine. Aurora isn't fine. She is out of the water. She's in a boathouse down the coast. The Vandermanns are paying to keep her there. The guy with the crewcut who sold her to me. Them. So sailing season is over. Probably over for you too. Got to get her out before your lake freezes over. Anyway, I biked down to visit her. The boatyard guys acted like I was in the way. But I didn't care. Somebody had to scrub her hull, bag the sails, tuck her in for the winter. I wanted them to know she's my boat. So they'll let me take her out in the Spring. Fingers crossed. Pray to St. Nicholas. So he knows what I want for Christmas. He's the patron saint of sailors. Yes, I know you knew that. You know lots of things.

Your cousin Anthony

Francis ditched his bike next to Anthony's in the dirt behind the bait shop. On the phone Anthony said he had secret stuff he needed to talk about. So did Francis. He'd had about as much as he could stand. "It sounds so friendly," said Francis. "Pop Warner. Like your dad is spiraling buttonhook passes right to the ol' breadbasket. Anthony, I'm telling ya, it's like boot camp without the boots. Mad at you if you're late, mad at you if you're slow, and really mad at you if you're not mean enough. They put half of your friends on the other team, then tell you to kill 'em, crush 'em, pulverize 'em. They can yell at me all day. I'm not gonna kill my friends."

"I'll sleep better knowing that," said Anthony.

"Yeah, like fun. I looked up this Pop Warner in the Britannica. I don't think he ever was anyone's pop." Francis picked up a pebble and pitched it with practiced aim through the mesh opening of the furthest lobster trap of the stack. "Rock lobster," he said. "Look, sorry I haven't been crew lately on Aurora. Did you replace me with another girl cousin?"

"I'm afraid not. That's what I wanted to talk to you about."

"Girl cousins?"

"Aurora."

After Anthony finished telling him all that had happened, Francis let out a big resonant burp, like he'd been holding onto it through the whole story. "Good one," said Francis.

After an appreciative pause, Francis elaborated, "They can't do that. Just 'cause the guy you bought the boat from was stupid?"

"Basically, yes. Though I don't think 'stupid' is a legal term."

"It oughtta be," said Francis, "and they should give Aurora back to you because you're less stupid than those Vanderpants."

"Vandermanns."

"Well, what are they going to do with it, your sail-boat?"

"I dunno. Dumped her at a boatyard. She's out of the water."

Francis picked up another stone, cocked back his arm. Then he just held it there, like he couldn't throw and think at the same time. "So. What are we going to do about that."

"We?" said Anthony.

"You know any other pirates?"

Out in the garden, Carol was scissoring the dead flower heads from the hydrangeas. In these last warm days you could still feel the approach of winter in the air. The end of the season.

Carol Vandermann couldn't make up her mind. She had very deliberately not looked at the sailboat that Steven had built, though that overly eager Mr. D'Ambrosio had tried to show her photos. She had seen what that boat had done to Steven's corpse, and that was enough.

She had sent Greg the first time. He tried to sell it off just to get rid of it. Somehow the kid he sold it to managed to get it into the water. Started sailing it all around the cove. So it could be anywhere. Which made it worse. And then this Mike D'Ambrosio began taking pictures and talking to everybody about boat design.

So she talked to a lawyer in town who'd helped
Steven with his patents. The lawyer said that who the
boat now actually belongs to is complicated. It's up
to a judge. But the boat design is clearly hers, though
there was no way to patent it. You can't patent the
shape of a hull. Steven's lawyer went to a magistrate
he plays golf with. Until ownership is determined,
and as practical protection against unauthorized
copying, the judge ordered impoundment in a
boatyard.

McCrudy's down near The Point. She could drive
over there and see it. Take a look. Since that phone
call from the town, it's been a revenant returned from
a saltwater grave. In the light of day, it might just become an ordinary sailing dinghy. Just another little
boat. But if it doesn't? When she saw it in the boathouse suspended above him, she knew that Steven's
life was in every inch of it. Now his death is also in
every inch of it. Once seen, there's no way to unsee
that.

⚓

"Dad, is Aurora still my sailboat?"

Anthony's father took a deep breath, the kind of breath adults take when they know that whatever they are about to say isn't going to be the least bit convincing. "It's a civil matter. At some point a judge will have to make a ruling." That deep breath again. "The town said that the Vandermanns had to remove the boat from public property. But wouldn't let them bring it over the town's protected dunes. So the Vandermanns were kind of stuck. Selling Aurora, so that somebody else would have to deal with her, was their only way out. So, they'd argue, the sale was compelled. Before they were able to realistically assess the true value of the asset."

"What's an asset?"

"Something you can turn into money. Like a house or a car."

"But Aurora isn't an asset," said Anthony. "She's my boat."

"I don't know, Anthony," said his father, and sighed in a way that kids never sigh.

Anthony thought about it. A lot. The guy who built Aurora didn't finish her. So she wasn't really a sailboat yet. She was some other kind of thing, an asset? Then Anthony attached the rudder. That finished the boat building. Like Anthony was partners with Steven the boatbuilder. But Anthony did it wrong. So what did that mean? Would a judge hammer his gavel on his big high desk and give his sailboat back to the Vandermanns because he botched it?

Whatever that judge was going to decide, Anthony knew what he had to do. Steven had loved this boat but had never sailed her. That felt unjust. Because Steven Vandermann was dead, Anthony had to do it for him. He had to finish Aurora. And do it properly.

But where do you get gudgeons and pintles? And how much do they cost? Anthony thought about his own assets. He had a pipe tobacco tin that rattled reassuringly when the coins clanked around inside, but that wasn't going to be enough. Allowance would take forever. He would have to find a job.

"I need gudgeons and pintles," said Anthony, "and I'm willing to work."

"Say what?" said Mr. McCrudy the boatyard manager, his Italian grinder sandwich halfway to his mouth.

"Gudgeons," said Anthony. "I can scrub the hulls on these boats. Or anything else you need done."

"Hunh," said the fat man and continued his lunch. Anthony stood there. He thought about all the convincing things he could say and said none of them. He watched the seated man eat. He watched him crumple the oil-soaked wax paper, watched him drop it back in the brown bag, and twist. Anthony stood there as the wrapper was tossed in a trashcan made from a marine fuel drum.

"You still there?"

Anthony stood his ground.

"Gudgeons? For why?"

"I need them for Aurora. That sailboat over there."

"You mean the one that got dumped here by that kid, Greg Wazisname?"

"Aurora. She's my sailboat."

"Well she sure ain't his, judging by the way he kicked her to the curb. You were the one who spruced her up, right?" The manager eyed Anthony over his substantial belly. "Gudgeons, hunh? Yeah. I think we can find stuff for you to do."

"I could start by sweeping the floor?"

"Don't." said Mr. McCrudy. "I'm paying you to work on boats. I'm not paying you to woman up the shed until I can't find anything."

So every Saturday in November and December Anthony bicycled over to the boatyard. And McCrudy always found plenty for him to do. Most of it was incredibly tedious, chipping and sanding the hulls of other people's boats, but Anthony didn't care. He spent his day surrounded by sailboats. Sometimes there were men working around him, repair guys or boat owners tackling some intricate task. Just as often, it was just McCrudy, stationary at his cluttered worktable, balancing his bulk on the rear legs of a chair.

Anthony only gradually noticed that how McCrudy paid him made no sense at all. Some days he was paid by the hour, some days by the job. And there was no way to figure what an hour or a task was actually worth because he was always paid for the full day at lunchtime, in cash, as they ate the sub sandwiches McCrudy ordered for them and drank Cokes from thick green glass bottles. Anthony worked harder in the afternoons.

But around 3:00 whatever Anthony was doing would be interrupted. It was always the same. "Jeez," said McCrudy, "you gonna just leave Aurora like that?"

So every Saturday from 3:00 until he pedaled home for supper, Anthony worked on his own boat. He studied the sailboats sleeping around him and, one by one, undid his earlier mistakes. He cleated the boom vang. He unscrewed the second-hand door hinges that held on the rudder. He ceremonially carried that rusted hardware to the empty marine fuel drum. McCrudy nodded as Anthony threw them in.

Carol made her decision. She drove her two-tone sedan to the boatyard. She would have a look. It wasn't like the boat wasn't already in her brain. Steven had wanted to show her a dozen times, but Carol had always found ways to beg off. She didn't want to see Steven's prize new sailboat in progress. Or rather, she lately realized, she didn't want to see how Steven gazed at this sailboat. She'd seen it in his eyes before, a kind of adoration, and it reminded her uncomfortably of when he raised her wedding veil.

Boys and their Toys didn't quite capture it. Makers and their creations? That made sense for the Integrated Wheelhouse, but this was something beyond that kind of male pride. She'd seen that look once, when Steven was crouched down working under Aurora's suspended hull, and that was enough for Carol.

But love, true love, isn't easy. It calls on you to accept more of another person than you can or that you want to. And sometimes it walks the grey line between what feels uncomfortable and what feels wrong. If there had been a mysterious woman in mourning at the graveside funeral, Carol would approach her. She would make eye contact through the black netting of her hat, extend her hand, and say with all the kindness she could muster, "Aurora, I presume."

She parked and pulled the handbrake. Tossing a floral scarf over her auburn hair, she tied it under her chin with a decisive knot.

McCrudy's Boatyard appeared to be a chaotic jumble of boats out of water: trailered outboards,

sailing yachts on their jack stands. But as Carol
walked among them a pattern started to emerge. The
least favored sat in the weedy outskirts, protected
only by discolored canvas covers and the squawk of
sentinel seagulls. Greg said he slid it off the rented
trailer into the weeds. But there was nothing out here
that could remotely have been Steven's Aurora. Carol
had a sinking feeling in the pit of her stomach. Somebody had moved the boat.

An inner circle of better boats was tucked under
the high davenport and windbreak of the boat shed.
Carol quickly excluded these aristocrats. There was
something vainglorious about them, like they were
built to make an impression. Dock yachts.

In the midst of it all were the rolling doors that
gave entry to the boathouse proper, fragrant with
sandpaper, varnish, and oily lubricants. As Steven
had taught her, that was always where the best and
the worst boats were kept, not just to be stored, but
to be restored, to be given new life.

Carol entered this workshop and she immediately saw Aurora. Amidst so many resting boats it
was startling how instantly her gaze was taken by Steven's creation. There was no question about it. Every

other sailboat became just so much lumber and cordage. There was nothing like Aurora, no comparison worth making.

Not that Aurora was pristine and shiny – far from it. Storm and shipwreck, abandonment and a season of adolescent banging about had left their marks. But to her surprise Carol could see beyond that to the beauty of its design, the sovereignty of its workmanship. There was more of Steven in herself than Carol had assumed. Even to a landlubber with a sea-queasy stomach a true sailboat will reveal itself.

Carol walked around Aurora hearing Steven's voice in her head. 'I extended the transom to…' 'Notice how the beam follows a natural harmonic ratio like the flanks of a fish…', 'The strakes confounded me for a spell, each one has to be bent three different ways.'

She circled around again to the stern. And stopped. The screw holes were clearly there. But the rudder was gone. Stolen. Or even worse. Borrowed. There was no other explanation.

A boat without a rudder. Carol had a very strong suspicion who might be responsible. That Mike D'Ambrosio. If he couldn't get the boat itself, he would take Aurora's lines. Now that the sailboat was out of the water he could slip in here and template every curve and angle. Above and below the water-line. There was no patent law to stop him. Once he stole the boat's lines, he could make a carbon copy, or a hundred. Pure piracy. He wanted Steven's de-sign, and apparently wasn't above taking it piece-meal, starting with the rudder.

There was no one in the boat shed except that big guy at the worktable asleep in his chair. But was he asleep? The chair was balanced on its two rear legs.

It was just the kind of place that Carol Vander-mann disliked. The scratched-up wood floor was splattered with spar varnish and big splotches of paint. Honestly, haven't these wharf characters ever heard of a dropcloth? The worktable was a disaster of tools and broken metal gizmos, the trash bucket spilled over. The boatyard owner fit right into his habitat, messy, which made Carol instinctively wary. Bay window belly slopping over belt buckle. Had he been otherwise she would have asked him directly about the rudder. Instead, she asked if he knew Mike D'Ambrosio.

"Yacht Club guy? Yeah, I've met him. Couple times."

"Recently?"

"Nah, they've got their own yard down the coast. Wouldn't have much call to come up here unless someone was looking to sell a boat. He'd be a good one to hook 'em up with a buyer." The boatyard guy cracked a crooked smile. "You know: the two happiest days in a boat owner's life."

"But he hasn't been here in the last couple of weeks?"

"Not that I've seen."

"So it wasn't D'Ambrosio who moved that sailing dinghy in here from the yard?"

"Nope," said McCrudy. Carol waited for more, but nothing arrived. Maybe she hadn't been clear enough.

"That one. The one with the missing rudder."

"Hunh. Hadn't noticed." Fat, sloppy, and dull-witted, thought Carol.

"So you don't know anything about it?"

"Nothing much, lady," said McCrudy, "'Cept one thing. That boat? It's Stevie Vandermann's."

Dear Anthony,

First of all, Lake Michigan does not freeze over. Never has.

Did you figure out that I was fibbing about tides? You were being a jerk when you said we didn't, so I said we did. I guess that makes us both jerks. So I'm kind of asking to forgive our trespasses. The Lake has tides, but they are so slight no one ever notices. What we do have is seiches. That's the wind piling water up against one shore and then when the wind lets up it sloshes back to the opposite shore. The cycle takes hours. A whole lot like tides.

I can't even believe that the Vandermanns have taken Aurora and put her in a boatyard. That stinks. Can your dad do anything about it? I'm glad that you can at least get in there and see her. With any luck the boatyard guys will forgive your trespasses.

Yes, our boat is out of the water. You probably know this, but a bag full of sails is a great place for mice to bed down for the winter. So don't leave them in the boat. If they'll let you take the sail bags away.

*I will pray to St. Nicholas for you and Aurora. I
will also pray to St. Brendan. He's kind of more the
saint of boatbuilders and navigators. Can't have too
many saints on your side.*

Your cousin Teresa

Carol Vandermann sat in her car with the windows
up and the motor off. The boatyard guy had shocked
her, recognizing Steven's boat. But why should she be
surprised? All these wharf characters know each
other, knew each other's business.

What Carol didn't know was whether McCrudy
had recognized her. Not that she'd ever seen him before, she was sure she would recognize a guy like that.
But her photo had been on Steven's boathouse desk,
right next to Melissa and Greg's school pictures. If
McCrudy was thinking at all, he must have put that
together. Who else would come looking for that battered sailboat? Which made it all pretty calculated,
calling her "lady", then dropping Steven's name like
it was common knowledge. This boatyard owner was

not someone you could trust, whatever Steven had thought of him.

Unless. Unless McCrudy had mistaken her for the mother of the kid. Whatsisname, Tony?

The kid's mother would be a good ten years younger than her. Carol tilted the rearview mirror, assessed the situation. She frowned into the reflection, then fumbled in her purse for her compact. Not likely. But not impossible, she decided, touching up her little image shining in the glass.

The mother would want to know about that Mike D'Ambrosio, trying to get his hands on her son's precious sailboat. That would make sense. But McCrudy hadn't said that he was wintering the boat for her kid. Assuming he knew he was talking to the mother, he'd gone out of his way to make it clear that the boat in question belonged to the Vandermanns. Which made sense. We are, after all, the people paying him to store it.

Who was she anyway, the kid's mother? What kind of mother would let her child take a sailboat off into the Bay, totally unprepared, prey to whatever weather was lurking out there? If his own mother wasn't going to protect her son from the sea, then

Carol would have to. The Aurora had already taken one life.

Carol realized she was being unfair. What do we know about other people's lives or families? She had little ground to stand on to judge another woman's child rearing. Greg was hardly a resounding advertisement for her skills. He still lived at home with no interest in ever setting foot in a classroom again, and no prospects of a job. But beneath that was her Bushy Bristle Bear who would do anything in the world for his Mom. And further down, beneath that, a little boy whose father is lost at sea.

She put the car in gear. She got halfway home, thinking about that guy at the boatyard. How he'd mistaken her for the kid's mother. Or had he? She turned the car around. She would put him straight.

When Carol arrived McCrudy was over by Steven's sailboat pointing out something to some woman. Carol instinctively knew that was the kid Tony's mother. A mother recognizes these things. Trying to get McCrudy to give the boat back to her son. As if we weren't paying good money to keep it here.

Well, she would put a stop to that. Carol marched herself over to the two of them and extended her hand. "Carol Vandermann."

"Yep," said McCrudy, shaking her hand with his big rough paw. "Good to see you again. So soon."

Turning to the woman, Carol said "I don't believe we've been introduced."

"I'm Lucy McConnell," she said. "That probably doesn't mean anything to you. I'm Anthony's mother. He's the boy who bought this sailboat."

"That's for the court to decide," said Carol.

"No. After my conversation here with Mr. McCrudy, I believe that matter is settled."

McCrudy grunted like he wasn't convinced of anything.

"I came down here to find out what Anthony is doing. You know as a mother that boys of that age can be secretive. I knew that he'd gotten a weekend job down here. I figured it was to be with his sailboat. He's been pretty attached. Like some boys put their baseball mitt under their pillow. But Mr. McCrudy here explained a couple of things I didn't know.

"My son doesn't just love sailing; he loves this sailboat. At first, he just wanted to sail it. Now it's something more, something maybe you can help me understand. He knows that you are taking it away from him because it was your late husband's creation. I am so sorry for your loss."

"Thank you," Carol Vandermann said dryly.

"And knowing that he came to this boatyard and got a job. I thought it was to be near this boat, and maybe he had some dream that he could earn enough money to buy it back. You know how unworldly young boys can be. But Mr. McCrudy tells me that Anthony is working to buy some kind of parts for your sailboat. Frankly this didn't make any kind of sense to me. It concerned me when I asked Anthony how much he was being paid per hour he couldn't give me a straight answer. And he used to have pocket change. You know, you'd sort it out of the laundry. Not these days. Every nickel goes in the tin. He even had to ask us for a postage stamp."

"See, he writes to his cousin Teresa, and that's another thing I'm a little concerned about. Kids this age can be secretive. So I told him I'd post his letter, and…"

"You steamed it open," said Carol.

Lucy averted her eyes, a mother caught in the act. "I did post the letter. But I made a copy. Because what Anthony wrote to his cousin really surprised me. I think it might surprise you too." Lucy opened her purse and brought out a neatly folded sheet of paper. She handed the paper to Carol.

This is what Carol read:

It's not my boat. When I get the rudder back on it, I'm gonna give it back to Mrs. Vandermann. Because I found out what Aurora is. She's the best part of her dead husband. The boat was unfinished. No rudder. So I have to finish the work. Because I know that if he had lived, that's what he would've done. And she had no name written on her stern. You probably noticed that. You notice lots of things. Mr. McCrudy said that the boat was a prototype for a new kind of sailboats, the Aurora class. But the name of the boat was never Aurora. He told me that Steven had already named her. The way mariners have always named their boats. The sailboat's name is Carol.

www.ingramcontent.com/pod-product-compliance
Lightning Source LLC
Chambersburg PA
CBHW011436240626
47153CB00011B/3015